EPITAPH FOR A LOBBYIST

By R. B. Dominic

EPITAPH FOR A LOBBYIST
THERE IS NO JUSTICE
MURDER IN HIGH PLACE

EPITAPH FOR A LOBBYIST

R. B. DOMINIC

PUBLISHED FOR THE CRIME CLUB BY
DOUBLEDAY & COMPANY, INC.
GARDEN CITY, NEW YORK
1974

All of the characters in this book are fictitious, and any resemblance to actual persons, living or dead, is purely coincidental.

ISBN: 0-385-08556-7
Library of Congress Catalog Card Number 73-9021
Copyright © 1974 by Doubleday & Company, Inc.
All Rights Reserved
Printed in the United States of America
First Edition

EPITAPH FOR A LOBBYIST

CHAPTER 1

Washington, D.C., is a city poised between past and future. What happens today in the Supreme Court or the Department of Agriculture shapes the tomorrows of millions of Americans. Next year's taxes, treaties, and elections are, after all, the stuff of government and politics. Presidents, ambassadors, and even typists grapple, day in and day out, with the uncertain future.

They do so in the shadow of the past.

For Washington is not only the seat of government, it is the embodiment of the nation's history. Monuments, statues, and pavilions, each part of a long roll of honor beginning with the Father of his Country, make modern Washington timeless.

"They're going to run out of space pretty soon," said Congressman Eugene Valingham Oakes (R-S.D.), leaving the Capitol Rotunda with Congressman Benton Safford (D-Ohio). Ceremonies commemorating a legislator whose portrait had just been presented to the nation, had finally come to an end.

Both delegates from the House of Representatives were appropriately solemn. But even while paying his respects to the late Senator Milleridge's daughters, Val Oakes had been preoccupied with hanging space. "Do you think these Rotunda people sneak some old pictures out of here every so often to make room for new ones?"

Ben Safford sensed that this was no passing interest.

"You expect somebody's going to be painting a picture of

1

you?" he suggested, following Oakes through the frozen mass of dignitaries.

Val was modestly complacent. "It's possible," he murmured. "No doubt contributions from the little schoolchildren of my beloved home state . . ."

Ben grinned. His distinguished colleague had a point. Congressman Oakes was a fixture in the House. More important, he looked like one.

Ben himself had no grounds for hope. The nondescript features that had kept him from being a young firebrand when he first entered Congress were, he expected, going to wash out his chances to pose as an elder statesman. Somehow or other, he did not see the schoolchildren of Newburg, Ohio (and the rest of his sprawling, 50th Congressional District) passing the hat for him. His respectable term in office proved that Newburg valued him enough to re-elect him, but that was about as far as he could go with Val Oakes. He did not expect any statues.

Future tributes, even if they are not problematical, do not occupy real pros for long, as Val demonstrated during their walk back to the House. Debate on the Floor still raged over the controversial Offshore Oil Bill. This afternoon would see an important session of the Joint Committee on Public Use of Public Lands.

"Then after that, there's this shindig Shirley Knapp's throwing, over at the NPA," Val summed up when they reached the Speaker's Lobby. "You going, Ben?"

He was asking about work, not play. Some cocktail parties promise rest and relaxation, but not this one. The NPA (National Power Association) was an influential special interest group financed by America's private power companies. Its guest list was strong on congressmen and senators. No district in the United States is unaffected by its local gas or electricity supplier.

Only society page editors could view an NPA bash as a congregation of simple fun-lovers.

Without asking, Val knew that Ben Safford had been invited. Picking and choosing from both branches of the Congress, not to speak of several regulatory agencies, might strain the ordinary party giver. But the NPA's eye was always on the ball. Every member of the committee that would report the Energy Expansion Act later this spring was sure to have received an impressive deckle-edged offer of hospitality.

"No, I'm giving the NPA a miss," Ben replied. "Mrs. Knapp is going to have to make friends and influence people without me."

Congressman Safford had served in Washington too long not to accept the local way of life while ducking some of its consequences. Banks, labor unions, corporations—and the NPA—maintained Washington offices expressly to make friends and influence influential people. Most of them had a legally registered lobbyist running the operation. The NPA's man in Washington happened to be Mrs. Shirley Knapp. She was one of the more high-powered members of a high-powered fraternity. Already this session, Ben had skipped an NPA banquet, declined NPA tickets to the Kentucky Derby and missed an NPA tour of interesting power installations—in the Caribbean.

Shaking his fine head, Val spoke with the frankness of an old friend. "I shouldn't be giving you tips," he said, "but I'll just pass on a lesson I've learned over the years. Remain true to yourself—and the folks back home—when you cast your vote. But in the meantime, never refuse free liquor."

Since he was an old political opponent too, Ben replied with another hoary adage.

"Val," he said, "there's no such thing as free lunch."

Hunger and thirst are not the only things that cut across party lines.

Ben was reminding himself of this later that day as he and Oakes stood clutching generous measures of the NPA's Bourbon and branch. Mrs. Shirley Knapp was hailing them like long-lost friends.

"Why, Ben! And Val!" she cried, pushing through the crowd. Her smile a mile wide, she sounded as if they were the two men in this whole throng she wanted to see. "And you've got yourselves drinks? Good!"

"It wasn't hard," Ben replied mildly. He had counted nine bartenders, all doing land-office business. "Shirley, I'd like you to meet Les Wilson. He's in town for a few days. Les, this is Mrs. Shirley Knapp."

Mrs. Knapp took one fast look, asked two key questions and,

within seconds, was leading Les Wilson off to meet a cabinet secretary.

"You're just the man he'd like to meet," she said enthusiastically.

Val nodded as the two moved away. "There now. That didn't take long. Shirley sure is quick off the mark."

"Too damned quick, if you ask me."

"She did what you wanted, didn't she?"

"She didn't have to be so smooth about it," Ben grunted resentfully.

For the last hour he had been the pawn of fate and he did not like it. Les Wilson was an old friend from home, in Washington on business. For two days Ben's secretary, Madge Anderson, had been on the phone insuring that various agencies were alerted to Mr. Wilson's arrival, that his hotel accommodations were satisfactory, that fashionable restaurants realized Mr. Wilson was no ordinary tourist. The red carpet had been rolled out. And Les had been grateful.

"Thanks a lot, Ben," he had said. "Everything went without a hitch, and I know it's due to you."

"You got what you wanted?"

"Yes sir, I got even more done than I hoped for." Les paused to shake his head. "But it's a funny thing, isn't it, how you can spend three days here in Washington without seeing even one of the famous people."

The wistful undercurrent would not have been lost on Safford even if Madge had not been sending up smoke signals from her place by the door. He knew that he could sit tight, wish Les a good trip and still score back in Newburg. But he also knew that Les's modest success would become a major triumph if he met just one of the people he saw on TV. And there on Ben's desk rested Shirley Knapp's invitation. Say what you would about the National Power Association, they always had celebrities coming out their ears.

"Hey, Les," he had heard himself saying, "if you could put off your flight a couple of hours, we could take in this cocktail party . . ."

This review was brought to a halt by Val Oakes.

"Now, Ben, I don't like to see you acting this way," he said sternly. "You came here because you wanted something from Shirley. She was smart enough to realize what it was and delivered for you. Instead of being grateful, you're complaining." He was struck by a sudden inspiration. "What you need is another drink."

Without further ado, he grabbed both glasses and headed for the bar. Unfortunately his departure gave Ben a clear view of Shirley Knapp doing her stuff with Congressman L. Lamar Flecker (D-Ala.). Mrs. Knapp was a small, vivacious, middle-aged woman. She knew exactly how each guest liked to have his roguish gallantry returned. She could be all business, she could swap dirty stories or she could blush. At the moment she was playing the Southern belle to Lou Flecker's Rhett Butler.

"For God's sake, Ben, stop looking that way," pleaded Val, who had fought his way back to find his colleague staring balefully. "I don't know what's gotten into you. You remind me of that fellow in the poem who kept barging in on folks having a good time and making them listen to the sad story of his life."

It was enough to divert Ben.

"I didn't know you read poetry, Val."

"I don't. But they made us all learn it when we were little. I don't remember anything except that line about not having a drop to drink." Reflexively, Oakes downed a healthy gulp.

Ben admitted that he had been brooding over Shirley Knapp's latest display of being all things to all men.

Oakes stared at him, glass suspended.

"I thought you were just feeling cantankerous at being forced to turn up here. But if you're seriously worried about Shirley Knapp fooling old Lou Flecker for one minute, then there really is something wrong with you."

Flecker had served on the same committee with Val and Ben for years. He was the wily and astute survivor of many political battles, a man who never put his foot down until he was sure of the ground.

"All right," Ben agreed. "I know Lou can handle ten Shirleys with both hands tied behind his back."

Just then, Flecker disengaged himself from Mrs. Knapp, aimed a broad wave and a half wink at his two colleagues and bore down on the federal commissioner he had been planning to buttonhole all along.

"See? What'd I tell you?" Oakes was smugly satisfied.

For Ben, the sight of Les Wilson across the room, happily chatting with a cabinet wife, was an additional tonic. "Oh, I knew all along you were right, Val. The fact is, these blowouts get me down. I don't like high-powered lobbyists and their greasy favors."

"Who does?" Oakes shrugged. "But they don't harm anyone with any sense."

"And the ones without?"

There was a lifetime of experience in the reply.

"Hell, Ben, the ones without any sense who come to Washington are going to find trouble around every corner."

Ben Safford was not going to make a fool of himself denying this kind of home truth. History was littered with too many cases in point. Instead, he decided to follow Lou Flecker's example and make good use of the NPA's hospitality. Within an hour he caught two men who never seemed to be available, let himself get caught by a third, and evaded an invitation from the District's most voracious hostess. He was momentarily confused when Oakes, taking a breather from his own chores, reverted to their earlier conversation.

"You should have held your fire, Ben. Now's the time to sound like an Old Testament prophet."

"About soy beans?" demanded Ben, still one step behind the music.

"No!" Oakes was impatient. "About Shirley Knapp! Look at the way she's doing her stuff now."

Mrs. Knapp had been backed against the wall by a man speaking earnestly. She listened in frowning concentration, apparently limiting herself to an occasional interjection. She had managed to dim her usual exuberance. In contrast, her companion was swelling with authority. Shamelessly Val Oakes edged closer.

". . . and not many people realize how complex these considerations can be."

Shirley Knapp was humble. "Of course, we appreciate having a real insider analyze the situation for us."

"Nonsense! I've always said that communication is part of a congressman's job. Now, you were asking what position I intend to recommend that the party adopt with respect to . . ."

The speaker took a deep breath.

"Of course, we both realize that no single individual always prevails in caucus," he declaimed, "but over the long haul I have found that my advice, more often than not, can be decisive."

Shirley Knapp could recognize a cue as well as the next woman. "With your years of experience, Congressman, that's not surprising."

A grave smile was her reward.

"Ah, experience! There's no substitute for it. We hear a good deal these days about the young rebels in Washington. But that's only for public consumption." He sighed tolerantly. "In private, I assure you, they know the value of an older head."

Ben Safford had heard too much. He propelled Oakes out of earshot, then said:

"Who is that windbag?"

"Come on, Ben. You must know Warren. He's been around long enough."

In a sense, Ben did. He recognized the face although he could not put a name to it. More important, he recognized the style. There was a band of nonentities in the House distinguished chiefly for inactivity. Unfortunately, they all looked alike. Short, rotund men with balding pates and anonymous features, they tended to be self-effacing with their colleagues. No wonder they let loose when they found a Shirley Knapp.

"I've been on a committee with him," Ben conceded. "A couple of years ago. He's from Nebraska or Kansas, isn't he?"

"It's old Warren Praeger. He's from Nebraska."

"I suppose he's yours, not ours."

Val agreed that the Republican Party could claim that honor.

"Well, one thing's for sure. Shirley Knapp has him eating out of her hand. Not that she doesn't pay a stiff price."

"You don't make enough allowance for the fact that Shirley's a woman. It's second nature for them to lay it on thick when they meet up with a Warren Praeger." Lazily Oakes surveyed the array of cocktail dresses brightening the room and cocked an ear to the tinkling laughs occasionally emerging from the background rumble. "I expect that most women are playing the same kind of game here."

Scarcely had the words left his mouth when the exception that proves the rule materialized from the throng. Congresswoman Elsie Hollenbach (D-Calif.), never played games. With iron gray hair, a ramrod back and awesome moral standards, she was both the scourge and delight of her colleagues. A tireless worker and a realistic legislator, she was about as flexible as a bulldozer.

"Ben," she said without wasting time on social niceties, "I've been wanting to have a word with you before Tony does."

"Is it about that pari-mutuel amendment that Tony is sponsoring?" he asked warily. Race track betting was sure to bring out the worst in Elsie.

"Exactly."

"Then look, Elsie. I'm about ready to leave now. Tony has already lined me up for nine o'clock tomorrow morning. Why don't you join us and we can hammer it out then?"

"Certainly, I myself am leaving now," replied Elsie, relentlessly falling into step with them. "But in the meantime, Ben, I would ask you to remember that the most depraved underworld elements are connected with illegal gambling."

She had more to say but she was cut off. Shirley Knapp was as alert to departures as to arrivals.

"Not going already, boys? Hell, the fun is just—" she began jovially before noticing the addition to the party. "Why, Mrs. Hollenbach, I didn't know you were here. What a shame our president wasn't able to get up from Texas. I know John wants to meet you."

Graciously, Elsie corrected her. She had met John Carrington a year earlier.

Being set straight did not bother Mrs. Knapp. "That's right," she said respectfully. "He was at that Berkeley Symposium where you made the keynote speech, wasn't he? I heard a lot of favorable comment."

Mrs. Hollenbach promptly unfurled a résumé of the Berkeley Symposium on Power Resources for the Future. According to her, it had been a valuable meeting and one she wished more people had been privileged to attend.

Ben was amused to note that Shirley Knapp was transformed into a serious student before their eyes.

"I wanted to take it in," she said soberly. "You know, we're just beginning to realize how important it is to educate the public about the coming energy crisis."

Not everybody could match Mrs. Knapp's absorption in Elsie's loftier statements. Certainly not Val Oakes.

"Isn't it about time we found that buddy of yours, Ben?" he broke in unceremoniously. "He's going to miss his plane."

In the scramble of extricating Les Wilson, listening to his almost tearful thanks and dispatching him to the airport, a general exodus was accomplished. But once they were in their own cab, heading back to the Hill, Ben realized that Mrs. Hollenbach had not surrendered the conversation.

"I shall send Mrs. Knapp a copy of my notes on the Symposium," she announced.

"You're not forgetting that Shirley is a paid lobbyist of the NPA, are you, Elsie?" inquired Oakes from the corner where he was slumped.

"Then it will do her all the more good."

Ben was amused. "Elsie, you deliberately inveigled Shirley Knapp into a position where she had to pretend to be interested in this symposium of yours. Now I suppose you intend to force her to read mountains of material," he said. "Not that she isn't asking for it, the way she turns herself inside out."

"I see no reason why I should not attempt to influence a lobbyist quite as thoroughly as she attempts to influence me." Some demon prompted Mrs. Hollenbach to expand this defense. "Besides, there is no reason to believe Mrs. Knapp was pretending an interest in the subject. She is, after all, a very efficient and competent professional. These are not qualities to be despised."

Val Oakes was not above a little malice. "Tony would tell you that you could say the same thing about a lot of Mafia employees."

Ben could feel Elsie Hollenbach stiffening. "I see no grounds for such an outrageous comparison. We all agree that Mrs. Knapp is employed by the private power companies. For all we know, Mrs. Knapp is sincerely committed to their cause."

"My father told me that most prostitutes don't have hearts of gold," Ben observed. "Myself, I wouldn't know."

High-mindedly Mrs. Hollenbach ignored this contribution. "The behavior of lobbyists is strictly regulated. Opinions on Mrs. Knapp's activities may vary, but she acts within the law."

"So far as we know," said Ben.

From the corner, there was yet another view. "I told you Shirley was a smart cookie."

Elsie retreated another inch. "Very well," she snapped. "At least you will grant me that Mrs. Knapp operates with tact and discretion. On that she cannot be faulted."

This opinion lasted less than twelve hours.

CHAPTER 2

When Ben Safford sat down to his bachelor breakfast in the hotel dining room the next morning, the first items in the newspaper to claim his attention were a large photograph of Shirley Knapp and a screaming headline.

WOMAN LOBBYIST LINKED TO BRIBE

$50,000 to Congressman

The Washington *Post* explained the underlying situation in three sentences. A year ago Congress had passed a law imposing air pollution controls on key industries. While the bill was being considered, a subcommittee of the House of Representatives had defeated a section making private power companies subject to the act. The vote had been five to four. Now, *a reliable source* had produced a memorandum by Shirley Knapp. Its first paragraph was damning:

> The vote to kill Section C will be 5-4. And believe me, that swing vote came expensive. The bastard wouldn't do it for a cent less than fifty thousand dollars. I know that's a big slice out of the slush fund, but I think you'll agree that it's money well spent. Section C would have cost us millions. And don't ask me if I could have gotten someone cheaper. Nobody else was even willing to listen.

Ben knew that several hundred congressmen were reading this story over their coffee and eggs. Charges of corruption against any member of the House send shock waves up and down both aisles. This morning there would be speculations, predictions and post-mortems in every office in the Capitol.

When he marched through the lobby he found two legislators already hard at it.

"I admit it looks bad," an old-timer from Chicago was saying. "But they haven't proved a thing yet."

"You're goddammed right they haven't," retorted the younger, savagely punching the elevator button for emphasis. "And why the hell should they? They can sell a lot of papers by just yelling rotten apple."

The speaker was a freshman member from New York City who had recently become a tenant of the Carlton. Ben had seen him frequently, but almost aways galloping for the airport limousine, overnight bag in hand. The straining tension of his hunched shoulders suggested that he had not yet learned any slower tempo.

The Chicagoan took a more relaxed view of events. The Washington *Post,* he said, was a reputable paper. They might be right, they might be wrong, but they had good grounds for their disclosure, you could be sure of that.

"That memo, by itself, is dynamite," he concluded. "It's as explicit as words can get. Still, the *Post* isn't going to have things all its own way. Just wait till Shirley Knapp goes into action, Herb. She'll turn this thing into a real dogfight."

Herb glared at his companion. He had an angular face with heavy brows now drawn into a horizontal black bar. "And a fat lot of good that will do!" he snapped. "Sure, the tabloids will love it if she drags things out all summer. But what about the rest of us? This kind of mud sticks. No! I say, make her cough up the rest of the dirt right now. I say—"

Further details of his battle plan were interrupted by the arrival of the elevator. A flying wedge of convention visitors split the two men apart and reminded Ben that the working day had begun.

Nonetheless, he spent the entire trip crosstown trying to remember who had cast those five critical votes.

He could have saved himself the effort. He arrived to find the

House buzzing. His own office already contained his secretary and two colleagues, engrossed in a welter of newspapers.

"We make it Gellert, Praeger, Macnamara, Isham, and Adelman," announced the small, dapper man by the window.

"Good morning, Ben," said Elsie Hollenbach, who liked to set a good example.

"Good morning, Elsie," said Ben obediently before plunging into the matter at hand. "I'll take your word for it, Tony."

The Honorable Anthony Martinelli (D-R.I.) was never wrong on questions like this.

"Poor saps. I wouldn't like to be in their shoes," he sympathized. "Make mine black with one sugar."

For the first time Ben noticed that Madge Anderson was busy with an enormous coffeepot. Although she was young, she was already a four-year veteran of Congress. That coffeepot was her forecast for the morning. It would never have appeared for a serious discussion of pari-mutuel legislation.

Now, carrying a cup and saucer to Mrs. Hollenbach, she set the ball in motion neatly.

"Everyone knew how Mr. Gellert and Mr. Isham were going to vote, didn't they?" she asked innocently.

This question needed no elaboration. Gellert and Isham had been voting against every conceivable form of federal regulation for over twenty years. Bribing them to do so would have been a waste of good money.

Tony Martinelli, gleaming from his patent-leather hair to his patent-leather shoes, was willing to put it into words. "So that leaves three of them—Praeger, Macnamara, and Adelman."

Spoon in hand, Ben looked up suddenly. "Which one of them is Herb?"

"That's Adelman from New York." Tony flicked lint from a silk sleeve. "He got in on one of those reform tickets. And he's in a hurry to reform everything in sight."

That certainly sounded like the impatient personality in the lobby of the Carlton. Ben pondered the list. He had seen Warren Praeger yesterday. And Richard Macnamara he remembered was one of the new-look suburban representatives who had been pouring into the House during the last four or five years. There had been a brief burst of publicity when Macnamara had proposed federal registration of snowmobiles.

Elsie Hollenbach, meanwhile, was endorsing Madge's analysis in her own stately fashion. "There would be small point in paying fifty thousand dollars for a swing vote unless there were already two sides. I am afraid you are right. Suspicion will inevitably center on these three men."

Ben saw a rare opportunity. "Well, Elsie," he inquired, "do you still think tact and discretion are enough to justify a lobbyist?"

There was not a moment's hesitation. When a Hollenbach position collided with a moral principle, it was the position that went.

"The whole affair is disgraceful," she said roundly. "I sincerely trust that we shall see criminal prosecution of both guilty parties."

"It'd be awfully hard to whitewash this one," Tony Martinelli agreed. "These lobbyists have been waving money around for years, but writing it all down on paper is something new. Why didn't Shirley just have a good heart-to-heart session with her boss?" Tony was saddened. "And I always thought that lady had her head screwed on right."

Elsie sniffed. "Lady is not the word I would use to describe Mrs. Knapp."

"Sure, sure." Tony was eager to avoid the lecture. "I suppose she'll try to talk her way out of it. But I'd like to know how she plans to do it."

John Bowie Carrington was asking himself this very question. Carrington was currently president of the National Power Association, the man who signed Shirley Knapp's checks, and the addressee of her now-famous memo. Alerted by a phone call, he was en route to his office at the national headquarters of the NPA in Houston, Texas.

But the man who stepped from the elevator into a maelstrom of reporters looked as if he did not have a care in the world. Tall and rangy, with a thick mane of white hair topping a tanned face, he combined formidable intelligence with a Texan's charm. Attentively he bent his head at the first barrage of questions.

"Did you get that memo?"

"Did the NPA supply that fifty thousand?"

"Was Mrs. Knapp acting on your instructions?"

Nobody was surprised at his reply. Smiling easily into the cameras, he said: "I'm afraid you're way ahead of me. I'm just back from a fishing trip and I haven't even seen the papers yet. You know, we get hundreds of memos from our Washington office every year. I think I'm just going to keep quiet until I catch up on what's going on."

"Are you denying that Shirley Knapp bribed a congressman to get Section C killed?"

"I have complete confidence in the integrity of Mrs. Knapp," he thundered. Then, less majestically, he continued: "She knows our rules and she's always stuck to them. Down here in Texas we believe in fair play. Why don't you fellas wait until you hear Mrs. Knapp's story before you start crucifying her?"

"Mrs. Knapp hasn't been giving us her story," yelped several reporters. "She's left Washington. She isn't available to the press."

This was news to Carrington, but he did not falter. Looking ruefully down at the crowd hemming him in, he said: "I don't know that I blame her. She's probably scared of being trampled to death. But seriously, I think she's wise to wait and make a formal statement."

Once safely inside his own office, he sang a different tune. "What the hell do we know about this goddam memo?" he growled, without preamble.

The face lifted to him was startled and apprehensive. "We don't know what actually happened. The Washington office handled Section C—"

Ruthlessly, Carrington cut off his assistant. "Don't tell me about the Washington office!" he commanded. "Tell me about this memo! How did the papers get hold of it? Have you checked our files?"

"But, sir!" the assistant protested. "We don't keep copies down here. You yourself told us to send everything from Mrs. Knapp straight to the shredder—"

"I know what I said," Carrington interrupted ominously. "I want to know if there's been a slipup. Have you checked the clerks? One of them could have pocketed it . . ."

"No!" the assistant cried, emboldened by absolute certainty. "That's impossible! I'm the only one who handles Mrs. Knapp's letters—after you've seen them. We tightened up procedures when . . ." His courage and the sentence ran out together.

"When Mrs. Knapp started getting so damned free with her pen," Carrington spelled it out. "I shouldn't have waited. I should have gotten rid of her then."

If you wanted to go on working for the NPA, you did not comment on any errors of judgment John Bowie Carrington might have made.

"Too late now," Carrington continued. "Let's see what we can do about the damage. Is it true that Shirley's dropped out of sight?"

"She hasn't been in the Washington office today. And when I called her house, her daughter told me that she took a suitcase when she left this morning."

The assistant expected an outburst but Carrington was soberly approving. "She's right to go to ground. It will give us a breather."

"I don't see what good that will do," the assistant said bleakly.

"I do. Shirley's got a real lively imagination. But she's got to tailor her story to fit the facts."

"Good God!" It was an involuntary interjection. "But it's the facts that are so—"

Carrington pressed on, unheeding. "Look, if the *Post* didn't get the memo from this end, then they got it from Shirley's end, right?"

The assistant followed that far.

"We-ell now." The drawl was exaggerated. "Then only Shirley can figure out where the leak was. Once she's done that, we can get together on a story that will cover it."

"But how can you get together when she's done a flit?"

"Oh, she'll be in touch." Carrington's confidence was fully restored. "And then we'll come up with something."

"You've heard the latest?" Val Oakes inquired while he waited next to Safford for the basement TV room, where both legislators were going to tape weekly messages for stations back home. "Shirley Knapp has skipped town."

"Maybe she's just lying low. I would."

"Nope." As usual Oakes heard everything without stirring from his office. "They've begun tracing her. She left home with a suitcase and her car's parked at the airport. She didn't buy a ticket under her own name. That's as far as they've gotten, but three guesses what she's up to."

Ben had no trouble with that one. "She's gone into a huddle with the NPA."

"That's going to be some huddle. I wonder what they'll come up with."

Val Oakes was kept wondering. Shirley Knapp did not return to Washington. Newspaper readers had to settle for a description of the Knapp household in Maryland. This included a substantial home set in manicured lawns, a nineteen-year-old daughter attending Thomas Jefferson University, her younger brother and a voluble housekeeper. For two days, this material had to do. Then, the wire services got into the act. It was an open secret, they stated definitively, that the safe in the NPA's Washington office had been stripped of cash.

"Not again," said L. Lamar Flecker, without a hint of the gay dog last seen at the NPA cocktail party. "I'm getting sick and tired of these safes stuffed with used hundred dollar bills. People back home are writing to ask me if there aren't any banks in Washington."

"Hold on, Lou," said Ben, who was going to withhold judgment if it killed him. "These stories don't say anything about how much cash the NPA actually kept in the safe. As for used hundred dollar bills—"

"They don't have to," Flecker shot back. "Not with Shirley Knapp passing out fifty thousand bucks."

"Allegedly," said Ben.

Flecker's sardonic look should have been comment enough, but he went on: "The NPA probably had $350,000 stockpiled. And don't tell me it was for polling purposes!"

Ben backtracked to the main point. "It still doesn't explain what's happened to Shirley Knapp."

Flecker snorted. "Maybe she's buying up the whole government of Uganda."

Flecker had spoken lightly. But, during the ensuing days, the NPA awoke to the danger of speculation along these lines. Accordingly, an official NPA spokesman held a press conference.

The whereabouts of Mrs. Knapp were still unknown. Rumors of missing cash were completely unfounded.

AP, UP and Reuters retaliated with a NPA stenotypist who had seen Mrs. Knapp stuffing a manila envelope with bills.

Before the spokesman could re-emerge, *Time* and *Newsweek* made him temporarily inoperative. The safe in the NPA office had indeed been emptied. But insiders in Washington and Houston confided that it had contained only paltry sums. "What you might call pin money," one source unwisely said.

This flushed thundering editorials and another appearance of the NPA spokesman, who was aging rapidly.

"To clarify an issue that has been raised," he said stiffly. "It now appears that Mrs. Knapp did withdraw approximately two thousand dollars from the NPA safe. At the moment, that is all the news we can give you on this subject."

Buzzing about the NPA safe kept all sorts of media pundits happily occupied. Radio talk shows, syndicated columnists and TV news-in-depth contributed to the snowball. Was the NPA accusing Shirley Knapp of robbery? Why did the NPA keep cash in its safe? What was Shirley Knapp doing with those used hundreds, and where?

"Naturally, the public wants to get to the truth of the matter," said Elsie Hollenbach as she rose from the table in the House dining room. "Ah, Ben! You know Dick Macnamara, don't you?"

A solid, athletic man, Macnamara was normally quietly self-confident. But he had the fair skin that goes with sandy hair and shows fatigue. At the moment, he looked punch-drunk.

"I don't pretend to follow this business about Shirley Knapp and that safe," he said wearily. "But no matter what the current NPA story is, it's out of their hands. You've heard that the Speaker has decided on a House investigation?"

"And quite right, too," Mrs. Hollenbach retorted. "The sooner this is cleared up, the better for all of us."

"Oh, I agree with that. I'd like to have the whole thing over tomorrow. But what kind of investigation can you have with the star witness missing?"

Mrs. Hollenbach was sympathetic, even after Macnamara left. "It isn't easy for any of them," she murmured. "Particularly now that all the commentators have narrowed the list down to three. And Dick Macnamara has his family right here in the middle of it."

"Never mind that," Ben said. "What's this about the Speaker?"

Elsie repeated her information. An investigating committee was on the brink of being formed.

"Macnamara's going to have a good long wait," Ben predicted. "First, Shirley will stay in hiding while the NPA decides the best way to build its case, whatever that may be. Then, the Speaker won't rush into naming the committee. And when he does, there'll have to be time for the staff to hold interviews and interrogate possible witnesses. When you have a House committee studying allegations that Shirley Knapp bribed a congressman, the one thing you want to avoid is turning the whole thing into a circus."

Elsie was a hard-core realist. "If it comes to a choice between charges of condoning corruption and charges of holding a circus, I believe I know how every member of Congress will respond."

"Every member of Congress," Ben reminded her, "except one."

CHAPTER 3

Ben Safford was wrong. There was no long delay; Shirley Knapp did not remain hidden; and when she made her appearance, it was not in Washington.

The news was flashed to the world at three o'clock in the afternoon.

"Shirley Knapp has been found," Madge Anderson rushed in to report.

Ben did not look up from his work. "High time," he grunted.

"In a hospital, no less," Madge continued.

"That's the latest dodge," said Ben, jotting a note. "Everybody in trouble seems to hole up in a hospital these days."

His secretary did not reply. Conscious of a break in the rhythm of their conversation, Ben glanced up. What he saw was enough to make him forget his pencil. Why was Madge looking so compassionate?

She took a deep breath.

"Mrs. Knapp has viral pneumonia at the Lavinia Finch Memorial Hospital—in Newburg, Ohio."

Ben barely had time for a premonitory shudder before the phone rang. Otto Buchak (D-Conn.) got down to brass tacks immediately.

"We're setting up that investigating committee right away." He paused awkwardly. "And, Ben, in view of your connection with Newburg, we're making you chairman."

Every politician knows when he is being handed a can of worms.

"Oh, no, you don't," Ben said crisply. "You're not saddling me with this just because Shirley Knapp turns up in Ohio."

Buchak had powerful ammunition at hand. "The Speaker himself suggested your name." He became confidential. "And he said he wouldn't forget."

Ben suppressed a curse. For all practical purposes, Newburg's urban renewal program had just been funded. But at what price?

He soon learned that things could have been worse. At least the composition of the Ad Hoc Committee was reassuring. Party stalwarts Tony Martinelli and Lou Flecker would sit across from the opposition, Val Oakes and Elsie Hollenbach. Within two hours they were all being briefed.

"You're going to have to drop everything else," Buchak began. "The way Shirley Knapp's handling this, there won't be any time for preliminaries."

Lou Flecker was skeptical. "Since when has viral pneumonia been such a crisis? She's not going to die on us."

"Two aspirins and a rubdown," Oakes rumbled knowledgeably.

"That's not the point. You've forgotten what a shrewdie that woman is."

"If she's so smart," Tony Martinelli protested, "how come her hideout's been fingered?"

"Good God, we didn't find her." Buchak sounded harassed. "She's the one who called the papers."

Martinelli stared. "She's holding press conferences? I thought she was supposed to be so sick."

"Let me start from the beginning. Her story is that she saw the Washington *Post* ten days ago and was very upset."

"She's got a winner so far," Val Oakes murmured.

"Wait until you hear how she goes on. She was so upset that she decided the wisest thing to do was seek guidance from her husband."

He was allowed to proceed no further.

"Her husband? Since when?"

"She's been keeping him pretty quiet, hasn't she?"

Otto Buchak swept on without answering any questions. "She flew to Newburg to talk things over with him. She was particularly concerned about their children. But she'd been under more of a strain than she realized. Almost immediately after arrival she collapsed and the husband rushed her to the hospital. For days she was isolated—no visitors and not even a television set. Yesterday she heard the radio and found out people thought she had fled from justice. So the husband calls in the local stringers and reads a statement. Now I want you to listen to this." He picked up a news release from the desk, hooked a pair of heavy horn-rims on his ears, and began to intone: "Mrs. Shirley Knapp insists that she has been defamed and demands the right to vindicate herself. She wants to know if the House is planning a real investigation or just an attempt to get headlines at her expense. She thinks it's extraordinary that she has to take the initiative in contacting us."

Buchak dramatically swept off his glasses and flung down the release.

"Short and sweet," said Tony Martinelli appreciatively. "Not a word about leaving Washington under a false name, not a word about any missing money from the NPA safe. You want to bet she was registered in the hospital under the husband's moniker?"

"Can I see that thing?" Ben demanded. He rapidly scanned the lines until he found what he wanted. "Mr. Charles S. Knapp, president of Knapp Contracting Corporation, told reporters . . ."

He looked up, blinking in puzzlement. "Who is he?"

Buchak was reproachful. "I thought you'd know for sure, Ben. This company he heads is right in your back yard."

"Never heard of him," Ben replied. "And I could have sworn that every contractor in town has been on my neck."

Buchak returned to the main issue. "Look at the predicament we're in. The House has been hollering that we want to talk to this woman and can't find her. Now she's hollering she wants to talk to us. If we don't get into action fast, the whole world is going to think we're pulling a whitewash job."

Everybody nodded.

"So the Ad Hoc Committee's going to have to go out to Newburg."

There was an incredulous silence. Then Val Oakes, easily the most resilient member of the group, reared up. "Now hold it, Otto. If she's out of the hospital, she can come here."

"Actually, she's not out of the hospital." Buchak grabbed for support. "But the doctors say her vital signs are good."

Someone snorted.

"We'd be playing right into her hands," Ben pointed out. "Shirley Knapp didn't call in the reporters until she—and the NPA—were good and ready. They've got a story worked out, but we won't be able to cross-examine her about it. Not if she's surrounded by tame doctors."

Oakes backed him to the hilt. "Think of the advantages you're giving her. If we go in there cold, we've got to take all this medical horse water seriously. The minute the going gets rough, she can say she's tired, she can act confused. Hell, she can faint dead away! You don't deal those kind of aces to a Shirley Knapp. She's already holding too many."

Even Elsie Hollenbach was in accord. "We would do better to wait until she's back in Washington. There are limits to how long she can spin out viral penumonia."

"Well, we're not going to," Buchak said with a ring of finality. "I've been talking to Wilbur and Phil."

At this reference to the powers who really ran Congress a stillness descended.

"And they don't like it any better than you do. But they say it's got to be done."

"Nice town you've got here," Tony said hollowly as the Ad Hoc Committee crept from its limousine.

Ben felt his responsibility for Newburg. "They've promised to have everything laid on for us," he replied. "Husband, doctors, everything."

"And what good are these people going to do us?" Lou Flecker demanded. "Whose side do you think they're on?"

A formidable array awaited them inside. In the welter of introductions Ben distinguished an NPA public relations man, an NPA lawyer, and a respiratory specialist from Houston. Surrounded by pin-striped suiting, Ben searched for the missing man.

"Where's Mr. Knapp?" he asked. "Isn't he here? I was assured that he would be present."

"Here I am!"

A man in work shirt and pants effortlessly brushed past two doctors. Striding forward, he extended a muscular hand.

"Charlie Knapp's the name, Congressman," he announced. "I know your sister."

At least that settled the problem of where to get background information on the Knapp family.

Charlie Knapp surveyed the newcomers with guileless blue eyes. "Glad you're here. Shirl's been wanting to get this over with."

As they jockeyed into the elevator, Ben was elbowed aside. A more hard-bitten interrogator took over.

"We didn't even know Mrs. Knapp had a husband until yesterday," Elsie began.

"Guess not."

"In fact everyone in Washington thought Mrs. Knapp was divorced," she fished.

Charlie gave this careful consideration. "Stands to reason," he said at last.

Congresswoman Hollenbach shifted tactics. "And do you live in Newburg?"

"Yup!"

"But Mrs. Knapp lives in Maryland," Elsie said with a wealth of meaning.

"That's right," he agreed readily.

Mrs. Hollenbach realized she had met her match. For one reason or another, Shirley Knapp's husband was not giving anything away.

Ben waited until Elsie retired from the field. "I hope your wife's condition isn't too serious," he said.

"Hard to tell."

It was not a promising introduction to Room 305 of the Lavinia Finch Memorial Hospital. Shirley Knapp, lying flat on her back, was almost totally obscured by equipment and nurses. Within seconds the doctors had joined the cast. One began taking her blood pressure, one conferred with the nurses and the third silently waved the visitors to a row of chairs.

Once these medical preparations were completed, the patient was propped up so that the Ad Hoc Committee could see its witness. Shirley Knapp's face was innocent of make-up; her lank hair was held back by a broad ribbon. She looked pale and defenseless.

The proceedings were opened by the specialist. Standing at the head of the bed, he advised his patient not to tire herself.

The PR man tried to punch the point home.

"Congressman Safford," he said gravely, "I am sure you understand that Mrs. Knapp, in her present condition, can only—"

"Clyde, baby," came the voice from the bed, "just shut up! We've already decided how to handle this."

"Oh, but—"

"Out!"

Clyde shrugged. "Just as you like, Shirley," he said, heading for the door.

The specialist did not give up as easily as Clyde.

"The room, in fact, is far too crowded." He scowled at the committee, now lined up like schoolchildren. "Surely it's not necessary to have all these people in order to ask a few simple questions."

Ben Safford would have been the first to admit that he was intimidated by hospitals and doctors. But sooner or later he was going to be forced into a show of authority.

"Dr. Barnes," he said as sternly as he could, "this committee has been charged with certain duties and we must speak with Mrs. Knapp. But not necessarily here and now. We have come, at considerable inconvenience, in response to Mrs. Knapp's request. For the record I wish to say that if Mrs. Knapp is too ill to testify, this committee is willing to withdraw until she can attend our sessions in Washington."

Ben did not expect to have his challenge accepted. But he was surprised to receive unexpected support.

"Attaboy!" said Shirley Knapp.

Ben pressed on: "Furthermore, we will not proceed without the consent of Mrs. Knapp, her doctor, her lawyer, and her husband. And the committee reporter will so note."

"Hey!" It was an involuntary exclamation from the corner. "But Shirl asked for you to come."

"That's all right, Charlie," his wife assured him. "First, everybody gives their okay, then everybody but the doctor leaves."

The NPA team exchanged glances that told Safford, plainer than words, that the script had already been rehearsed.

The lawyer put up only token resistance. But, after the general exodus Ben was dismayed to find that this exchange had taken its toll. Shirley Knapp was breathing faster and her voice was now a thin thread.

"Are you certain, Mrs. Knapp . . . ?" Ben began.

"Yes. I want to get this on record." The words were coming through clenched teeth.

The formalities of oath-taking were soon over.

"Mrs. Knapp, perhaps it will save time if I ask if you have seen the Washington *Post* of June third?"

"Yes."

"The front page contained what purported to be the text of a memorandum written by you to John Carrington. Do you remember that front page?"

"I do."

"The Washington *Post* tells us that they have a copy of this document signed with your initials. Do you have anything to say?"

Shirley Knapp had been saving her energy for this moment. In a much stronger voice, she said: "I sure do. It's a forgery. Those aren't my initials."

"And the text of the memorandum? Do you repudiate that also?"

"I never dictated such a memorandum in my life!"

Ben again bypassed technicalities. "Never mind the dictating. Did you contribute to such a memorandum in any way? Did you compose it or did you type it?"

"I did not. The whole thing is a forgery from beginning to end. I intend to sue every newspaper that published it."

She sounded sincere, but sincerity is part of a lobbyist's stock-in-trade. More important, she sounded confident. Ben had not anticipated this kind of defense, but Shirley Knapp knew what she was doing.

Especially after shredding machines in Washington and Houston had been working overtime.

The frown on every face told Ben that he was not alone in seeing shoals ahead. He continued:

"Mrs. Knapp, let's leave the memorandum for a moment. Have you bribed any member of Congress—specifically any member of the Gellert Subcommittee—to vote against Section C of the Industrial Pollution Bill?"

"I have not, and anybody who says that I have is a liar," she said loudly enough to make the doctors stir.

A hospital room is not the best place to remind witnesses of perjury penalties. Moreover Shirley was sure of herself. Ben knew what would happen as soon as she was not.

"I would like to speak with you about your relations with Congressmen Adelman, Praeger, and Macnamara."

Shirley let her head loll back against the pillows. "Go on," she whispered.

She was forcing him to spell it out. "I am sure that you must have spoken with them during the deliberations on Section C," he said.

"Yes," she said weakly, as if this required all her strength.

This performance evoked varied reaction from the rest of the committee. Tony Martinelli, bright-eyed with interest, might have been at a superbowl. Elsie Hollenbach was taut with displeasure. Lou Flecker shifted uncomfortably while Val Oakes seemed sleepier than ever. But it was Val who fatalistically shook his head in response to Ben's silent SOS. They could all see what was coming.

"We'll take Congressman Adelman first," said Ben doggedly. "Will you tell us about any private meetings with him?"

Shirley pressed both hands flat against the bed as if she were about to struggle erect. "I'll try," she gasped gallantly. "What do you want to know?"

"How often did you meet him alone in the last two weeks of deliberation?"

There was only one maneuver left for her. "Congressman Adelman and I . . ." she began, before suddenly choking and clasping both hands to her chest. The doctors swarmed forward, the nurses converged on the equipment and the bed disappeared from view.

But not quickly enough to prevent Ben from seeing the mocking glint in Shirley Knapp's eye.

"She planned it that way," he growled two hours later. "We didn't have any choice."

The rest of the committee had already left Newburg. Ben was spending the night in the big old house on Plainfield Road.

Right now, his sister Janet was listening sympathetically. His brother-in-law, Fred Lundgren, was refilling his glass.

"Then you did the only thing you could, and there's no point in worrying," Janet remarked placidly.

"Not worry? Hah!"

"You said yourself that even Val couldn't think of anything to do."

It was received truth in the Lundgren home that Oakes was the consummate politician in Ben's immediate circle.

"Nobody in the hospital could think of anything to do," Ben retorted. "Wait until the Monday morning quarterbacks get to work."

"Not in Newburg, they won't!" Janet did not have to remind him that it was the Newburg quarterbacks who elected him. "Everybody here is thrilled to have the town—and you—in the limelight."

Ben was deriving comfort, either from his sister's arguments or from his second drink.

"I suppose so," he grumbled. "But it's going to look a lot different in Washington."

Fred had been too busy dispensing hospitality to follow the discussion closely. "I don't see what the big problem is," he complained. "You wanted to find Shirley Knapp. You've found her and she's yelling forgery."

Ben leaned back, cradling his glass in both hands, to explain. "If she made that claim on the witness stand in the House Office Building, we would have gone over her story for days. We'd have concentrated on her dealings with the three congressmen, we might even have uncovered how she laundered that fifty thousand. But where do I go from here?"

"The Washington *Post?*" Fred nodded thoughtfully. "I can see how you don't like that one."

"Exactly. You know how newspapers feel about revealing their sources. But we've got to establish the authenticity of that memo. So, before we know it, we'll be in front of the Supreme Court."

There was only one thing to say and Fred said it. "She's smart, all right. How long do you think it took her to work this one out?"

Janet was frowning as she passed a tray of cheese and crackers.

"But even smart people make mistakes. Would it do any good questioning the staff in her office?"

"Absolutely none," Ben said without hesitation. "Shirley would never have risked it otherwise. That's what she's been making up her mind about. When that memo burst into print, she didn't know what had hit her. She had to review her office procedures and spot the leak. Only when she was certain of not being contradicted did she decide to claim forgery. But figuring out the odds took time and she needed a place where nobody would look for her. That's why she flew to this long lost husband." Ben was reminded of a grievance. "And who the hell is Charlie Knapp anyway? He says he knows you."

"Of course he does." Janet was complacent. There were not many registered voters in Newburg County who did not. "He did our driveway last year. Charlie owns a small blacktopping outfit."

What Janet knew about Newburg's personnel, Fred knew about its businesses. Between civic activities and the Lundgren Ford Agency they made a powerful team. "Not such a small outfit," he corrected. "You know Charlie did the parking lot of that new shopping center over in Curryville. And he's got a bid in for the municipal tennis courts. He's making a good thing out of blacktopping."

"Has he been around long?" Ben asked.

"Years and years," Fred said cheerfully. "Charlie's a real character. I know he's big in the Rotarians and I've bumped into him myself at the Chamber of Commerce dinners."

"Didn't you know he was married?"

"He certainly never mentioned it."

Janet allowed herself a touch of malice. "I wonder if he mentioned it to Edwina Mills."

Ben's eyebrows lifted inquiringly.

"Charlie likes to step out with the ladies," Fred grinned. "And Edwina has been a widow for three years now."

There was nothing unusual in any of these details. Charlie Knapps exist in every American town. But the skeleton in their closet is rarely a powerful Washington lobbyist.

Ben was still after information. "I suppose Charlie hasn't told you why Shirley showed up here?"

"No," Janet confessed with some chagrin. "When he called last night to ask about you, I hinted around until I was ashamed."

Fred was triumphant. He rarely beat Janet at her own game. "He told me," he crowed. "When he came in for a headlight today."

Janet was incredulous. "How in the world did you get him to talk about it?"

"I asked," Fred said simply. "She walked out on him fourteen years ago. The first time he saw her again was when she rang the doorbell last week."

It took a moment for his audience to recover.

"Did he tell you anything else?" Janet asked faintly.

"If you call it that." Fred's teeth glinted. "He said he was awful surprised."

"I told you she'd stop at nothing," Ben said. "Wait until she's through. She'll be a persecuted innocent crying for justice."

Janet's eyes narrowed. "That may be true in Washington, but there's no reason you can't get in first here in Newburg."

Thanks to his sister's feelings about seizing the day, Ben was inured to a full speaking calendar whenever he set foot in Ohio.

"I have to go back tomorrow afternoon," he said quickly. "And I'm seeing the boys at the UAW in the morning."

"Certainly. But tonight you can speak to the Grange. It will make a very nice audience for you. And," she said, throwing in the clincher, "it will get complete coverage in the Newburg *News*."

CHAPTER 4

In Washington, there was no question of Ben Safford's getting in first. Others were there ahead of him.

"You have a visitor, Congressman Safford," Madge Anderson announced the next afternoon. "Alison Knapp."

"What!" Ben was taken aback. For years there had been only one Knapp on the horizon. Now, wherever you went, they sprang up at you.

"The daughter," Madge explained.

"Oh God!" Ben could already see the headline: GIRL PLEADS FOR STRICKEN MOTHER.

Madge read him like a book. "It's even worse than that. Wait till you hear what she's got to say."

"All right. Show her in," he said, reminding himself that in two years Alison Knapp might be a registered voter in Ohio's 50th Congressional District.

Right now, she was a coltish blonde trying valiantly to look at ease.

"Well now," Ben said, "what can I do for you?"

"Didn't she tell you?" Alison was unhappy at having to explain again.

Ben made a neutral sound of encouragement.

"It's about this." Alison produced a newspaper account of yesterday's scene in the hospital. She shot an uncertain glance across the desk. "My mother claims that memo about the bribe is a forgery. And now people say you're going to let it drop there."

"I'm afraid it's not that simple," he said gently. "We'll start out by talking to the *Post*."

"Oh, you don't understand!" she cried. "I'm the one who stole the memo!"

Ben gaped and hastily readjusted his thoughts. "*You!*" he repeated. "Then how did it get to the *Post?*"

"I gave it to them."

Ben struggled for a foothold. "Maybe," he suggested warily, "you'd better go back a little. When and where did you get hold of that memo?"

It was not the facts that troubled Alison. "It must have been over a year and a half ago," she began. "Anyway, it was before the vote on Section C. My mother's always done a lot of work at home. One night I was using the phone in her study and there was some stuff on her desk. I had to hold on for a couple of minutes and I just happened to read the top carbon." She came to a full stop.

"Go on," Ben said.

This was harder for her. "I couldn't really believe it," she blurted. "At first I thought it was a put-on, just Mother trying to sound tough the way she does. Then the vote was exactly what she planned, but it was too late for me to do anything."

"Why?" Ben asked sharply. "Why was it too late? You could have gone to Chairman Gellert."

Alison avoided his eyes. "Actually, I didn't find out what happened to Section C until later on."

Ben was suspicious. "What do you mean by that?"

She blushed. "I was starting college that year. I had other things to think about besides crooked politicians."

"And when did you find out that Section C had been defeated?"

"Not until six months later," Alison confessed. "Somebody mentioned it as a good example of how the fat cats operate."

Ben leaned back and crossed his legs. It was not hard to imagine what had happened last year. Eighteen years old and absorbed in her new life, Alison had simply forgotten all about the dynamite she had taken from Shirley Knapp's desk. By that time, the Industrial Pollution Act—minus Section C—was the law of the land.

"That takes us to last spring," he commented. "You decided it was too late to do anything. Why the about-face now?"

Alison drew herself up and looked steadily forward. "Because it was starting all over again. The NPA was interested in another bill. If there was a repeat of this corruption," she said earnestly, "I'd share the guilt this time. The people who remain silent about a massacre are as morally culpable as the people with guns. So I went to the *Post*."

Ben digested this helping of the new morality, then fell back on the old.

"I can't promise anything," he began guardedly, "but it may not be necessary to call you as a witness."

"That's all right," she said bravely. "I went to the *Post* this morning and talked it over with them."

Ben blinked. "And you're willing to testify before the committee in open session?"

"Yes," she gulped.

Did she realize that she might be sending her mother to prison?

It was impossible to tell. But, even if Ben did not understand Alison Knapp, he recognized that she was doing a fine job pulling his chestnuts out of the fire.

The chestnuts, of course, reacted differently. Within twenty-four hours, three congressmen had given Ben Safford the benefit of their advice about the future course of the Ad Hoc Committee.

Warren Praeger (R-Neb.) wanted the hearings postponed.

"No," Ben said for the last time. "The hearings will continue on Monday. I have already told John Carrington to be ready."

Shoulders sagging, Praeger turned for a final word. "I didn't expect this, Ben, not from one old-timer to another. But I happen to be having dinner tonight with the Speaker. I guess I'll just have to go over your head."

Let him find out for himself, thought Ben, that it was the Speaker who was urging the committee forward.

Herb Adelman was more forthright. The Knapp family was leading the committee by the nose. The questioning in Newburg had been bungled. Shirley Knapp should have been forced to divulge the name of the man she had bribed.

"I can see you've got a lot of objections to the way this committee is being run," Ben said in an attempt to cut the catalog short.

"You're damned right I do!" Adelman said bluntly. "I'm going to New York this afternoon to see my backers. And they're going to want to know why we're horsing around down here."

Dick Macnamara (D-Mass.) believed in the casual approach. He arranged to run into Ben in the corridor where he outlined an elaborate plan for restructuring the hearings. The rights of at least two innocent congressmen were at stake. They should have advance notice of witnesses called, they should participate in cross-examination, they should . . .

"That's quite an idea, Dick," Ben said unenthusiastically. "I'll think about it."

Macnamara was unwilling to leave it at that. "I hope you will, Ben," he said. "Look, I've got to run over to a convention right now. But we could get together tonight. I'll be working here on the Housing Bill, anyway . . ."

Alison Knapp had really brought things to a boil, Ben reflected as he escaped back to his office. Three congressmen could feel the pressure mounting, and three congressmen were reacting differently. But they had one thing in common. Warren Praeger, Dick Macnamara, and Herb Adelman each felt it expedient to keep his nose to the grindstone this Friday evening.

"Now, Mildred, you know I wouldn't duck out," Warren Praeger was saying some time later to his wife. "I'll be there in about an hour."

They were standing in the foyer of their apartment. Patting her hair in front of the mirror, Mildred objected: "The invitation said six o'clock."

"Oh, they won't go into dinner until seven-thirty at the earliest."

"But, Warren," she protested, "I always think it's so nice when you and the Speaker have time to get together."

"That's true, Mildred, but you'll just have to explain that something came up at the last minute." He drew himself erect. "The Speaker understands about putting business before pleasure."

Mildred was rooting through her evening bag. "I suppose so," she sighed. "But it seems such a shame."

Praeger stood with one arm arched behind his wife as if ready to sweep her out the door.

"For goodness' sake, Mildred, what are you looking for now?"

"My key," she said disentangling a comb and handkerchief. "I'll need it if—"

"No, you won't," he said patiently. "I've already told you, I'll be there in an hour."

Fortunately, just then, the key emerged from beneath a compact. After his wife bustled off, Praeger pulled out a handkerchief and mopped his brow.

At the same time, Herbert Adelman was entering the Carlton. The desk clerk looked up in surprise.

"Mr. Congressman! We thought you were spending the weekend in New York."

"I changed my mind," Adelman said flatly.

The clerk plucked some mail from a pigeonhole with dignity. You never could tell, he thought. Most permanent guests were delighted if the staff displayed familiarity with their habits.

"I'm afraid the maid hasn't been up there this afternoon. I could send someone up now," he offered.

"No!" The single word came out too forcefully. Apologetically, Adelman added an explanation. "I'm going to be working tonight and I want to get right down to it."

"Certainly, sir."

Adelman was turning toward the elevator when he thought of something else. "If anyone calls this evening, tell them I'm out. I don't want to be bothered."

The clerk knew a great deal about the Adelman family.

"Does that include . . . ?"

"It includes everybody."

Even Dick Macnamara changed his plans. At 6:30, when his wife pulled a station wagon into the driveway, he was in sports shirt and slacks, mowing the lawn.

"Dick!" she exclaimed. "I thought you were spending the evening at the office."

"So did I," he agreed. "But I had a hell of an afternoon. First, I had to show up at the National Landmarks Convention. Then

I got stuck with a bunch of people from back home. By the time I shook free, I decided a night off wouldn't hurt."

"What a shame Friday's my Red Cross day. There isn't anything but leftover stew," she said.

It was a hot day and the lawn was substantial. Kate Macnamara viewed her husband's perspiring face and felt a twinge of compassion. But in fifteen minutes, the children would return, clamoring for attention.

"You could run down to the Smiling Buddha and get something to take out," she suggested tentatively.

"Oh, no, you don't. I didn't take time off to drive five miles and stand in line smelling soy sauce. I'm not going anywhere." He underlined his point by leading the way to the porch and flopping into a chair. Then he linked both hands behind his neck and stretched luxuriously. "It's great to be home."

"Great to be home!" echoed two couples straggling into National Airport with deep tans and string bags filled with Caribbean loot.

But it had been wonderful to be away, too, they agreed. Imagine having to go all the way to Puerto Rico to meet each other. The bond cementing the group had originated in the discovery that both men were dentists, both took Mondays off, and both had difficulty finding weekday golf partners.

They were deep in discussion of nearby courses as they trudged toward the garage. By the time they reached the first car, they had almost settled on Indian Spring Country Club.

"That woman wants to back out," one of the wives remarked.

They all moved farther aside and agreed to add dinner to the schedule for Monday. Then there were hearty farewells and the car door was swung open.

The driver had one foot inside and was peering directly across his front seat. "Say, isn't she ever getting out?" he complained.

The bright strip lighting of the garage failed to penetrate interiors. All they could see was the shadowy outline of a woman bent over a steering wheel.

The wife circled the car. She turned and rapped briskly on the woman's window. There was no movement.

"George," the wife said tautly. "I think something's wrong."

But both men were already at her side, tugging at the door handle. Before they understood what was happening, the silent figure swayed forward into their arms.

"Oh, my God!" moaned George. "Half her head isn't here!"

"Put her back," half screamed the other dentist, fighting back nausea.

Clumsily, they managed to replace their grisly burden and clamp the door shut.

The wife, her eyes carefully averted, stooped to pick up a wallet.

"Here," she said dully, "this came out, too."

George had his back pressed to the door as if he were afraid it would reopen. He was thankful to look at anything else. After one glance, surprise began to replace horror.

"But this says Shirley Knapp!" he exclaimed.

CHAPTER 5

The police moved fast. Within half an hour they established two facts. The dead woman was Shirley Knapp; she had been shot to death in her own car. In short order a section of the airport garage was cordoned off, the body and the car were removed, and an army of plainclothesmen fanned through the terminal.

"I'll say one thing for this mess," growled Captain Rudolph Heyer. "At least with Shirley Knapp we don't have to dig for background."

It was now 8:30 and the technical reports were not due for several hours. But nontechnical details were pouring in.

The first information came from Newburg, Ohio. Shirley Knapp had spent yesterday resting comfortably at the hospital. This morning she had wakened late, turned on the radio, and learned of her daughter's revelations. Then John Bowie Carrington had phoned from Washington. Mrs. Knapp's side of the conversation, according to her nurses, was a steady stream of profanity. Immediately after hanging up, she had announced her decision to quit the hospital. Over the protests of her doctors, she had left at one o'clock under the escort of her husband. Charlie Knapp's phone was not answering and the Newburg police had no idea where he was.

American Airlines, however, reported that a Mrs. Shirley Knapp had traveled alone, on Flight 307, arriving at National Airport at 4:38 P.M.

Headquarters had produced a précis of news coverage on the murdered woman's last two weeks. It gave him names, dates, figures—and three ready-made suspects.

"Congressmen, yet!" he said, deciding to start with Shirley Knapp's office.

Captain Heyer had read enough about shredding machines not to expect much. But, when he found the lights blazing late in the NPA suite, he began to wonder.

The outer office was deserted so he rapped sharply on the receptionist's desk. There was a flurry of movement, hasty steps, and a peremptory voice:

"Where the hell have you . . . ?"

The man with a leonine head stopped himself when he saw the police uniform of Heyer's driver.

"Expecting someone?" Captain Heyer asked.

There was no answer. The man examined his visitors, looked past them to make sure they were alone, then plucked his lower lip.

Heyer recognized the breed: the kind who think before they talk.

"I'm Detective Captain Heyer," he said, hoping to speed things up.

"What's the trouble? What are you doing here?"

Heyer could ignore questions, too. "Who are *you?*" he retorted.

This simple query was studied from every angle. Then: "John Carrington. I'm President of the NPA. What—" He would have continued but he was interrupted by the footsteps of a woman hurrying down the corridor. He pivoted tensely toward the door, then relaxed when he saw who it was.

"This is Mrs. Barbara Underwood," he explained. "She was kind enough to go out for some sandwiches."

Heyer remembered the précis. "You're Mrs. Knapp's secretary, aren't you?"

"Not secretary. Administrative assistant." She was piqued at his error.

Captain Heyer liked witnesses who wanted to correct him.

"Expecting Mrs. Knapp?" he asked her.

"Yes, but she's late . . . that is . . ." Mrs. Underwood's voice trailed away as she caught Carrington's warning glance.

"Why don't we all sit down and talk about it?" Heyer suggested.

But John Carrington had different ideas. "Not until I know what this is about," he said. "If you're not willing to tell us, you'll have to leave."

Heyer decided to try shock tactics. "Shirley Knapp's body has been found—with two bullets in her brain."

There was a stunned silence. Mrs. Underwood pressed trembling hands over her mouth. Carrington blinked, his body unnaturally still.

"My God, that's terrible," he said at last.

His shoulders twitched unconsciously as he looked around. For the first time he seemed aware they were standing in a vast reception area, their voices sounding hollow against the backdrop of vacant desks and couches.

"Let's get out of here," he said. "There's a room in back we can use."

He led the way to a small office.

Barbara Underwood rushed to unplug a thumping percolator. "I forgot all about it," she said. "I started the coffee before I went out."

"We'll all have some," Carrington directed.

By the time they were served, Carrington had made up his mind. First he asked if Shirley Knapp had been the casual victim of a street crime.

"No," Heyer said positively. "She was shot in her own car at National Airport. And no money was taken."

"So she did come." Carrington nodded to himself. "You asked if we were expecting her, Captain. She was supposed to be here at seven o'clock. By the time you came, I didn't know what to think."

"You knew she was out of the hospital?"

Carrington was frank, up to a point. "I spoke with Shirley this morning," he said easily. "She was feeling a lot better and planned to come back to Washington. After this story from her daughter, I thought we should have a talk. We agreed to meet here at seven."

Heyer let this pass. The first round was no time to press Carrington about that stream of profanity.

"And you weren't worried when she didn't show up?"

Carrington met his eyes squarely. "I was worried all right, but about the wrong things. Now, Captain, I don't deny that Alison Knapp's story shook me. Until then I had implicit faith in Mrs. Knapp. By the time I called her this morning, I had grave doubts and I wasn't hiding them. That's why I wanted to see her face to face. When she didn't turn up here by seven-thirty, I called the hospital. She checked out at lunchtime. For all I knew she was already in Brazil."

Rudy Heyer knew that he was getting a preview of the new NPA line on its Washington lobbyist. Because in Carrington's world, politics took priority over murder. And Heyer foresaw that this would be true for almost every one of his witnesses.

For the police, however, murder still took first place. "Why didn't you follow up the hospital call with a call to the airlines?" Captain Heyer asked. "If they told you she wasn't on her flight, you would have known she wasn't coming to Washington."

Carrington denied knowing what flight, or indeed what airline, Shirley Knapp intended to use. Their only arrangement was the seven o'clock meeting. He was even less helpful on the subject of an alibi.

"I spent most of the afternoon on the Hill talking to Senator Brewer. Then I went back to my hotel about four-thirty. I was going to rest up and have some dinner. But to tell the truth," he grinned ruefully, "I ended by taking a nap. I work up just in time to get over here by seven."

Heyer turned to Barbara Underwood. Secretaries, he had found, could be as bad as relatives. Some of them would turn themselves inside out for their bosses. So he began cautiously.

"You've been administrative assistant to Mrs. Knapp for how long, Mrs. Underwood?"

"Two years."

"Then you knew her pretty well?"

"To a certain extent."

"I mean in her professional capacity."

"I don't know anything about her trying to bribe congressmen," Mrs. Underwood said swiftly.

"I guess I'm not making myself clear. You'd have a good idea of how she'd react to this morning's paper, for instance?"

Barbara Underwood's careful neutrality slipped. "She'd be furious," she said with open satisfaction.

"And she'd want certain things done. Did she call you and ask you to do anything? Or did you call her?"

The curtain went down again. "I have not spoken with Mrs. Knapp since she left Washington."

Heyer persisted. "Then how did you hear about the seven o'clock appointment?"

"I happened to be working late when Mr. Carrington arrived at seven. He told me then."

"And very happy I was to find Mrs. Underwood," Carrington said gallantly. "I wouldn't have dared ask her to come back, not when she's been holding the fort alone."

Nevertheless, he had asked her to wait with him through the subsequent vigil. They had been together until shortly before the police arrived when hunger overcame Carrington.

Mrs. Underwood's account of her earlier movements was less helpful. She had left the NPA during the tidal wave between 5 and 5:30, stopping for a sandwich and coffee at a cafeteria three blocks away. Then she had gone to a lingerie store on Connecticut Avenue to buy pantyhose on sale. On returning, she had signed the elevator list at 6:30.

"Thank you very much," said Heyer. "I guess that just about wraps things up."

Carrington stared. He had been braced for questions about fifty thousand dollars, about bribery, about the name of one greedy congressman.

But Captain Heyer could think of better places to ask them.

A report was waiting when he reached the squad car. "Only one of those three phones answers, Captain," headquarters told him.

"Well, that settles where we start," Heyer said. "You've got the address?"

At Winterberry Lane in Bethesda, Maryland, Congressman Richard Macnamara answered the doorbell himself. With a flare of alarm, he asked: "Has there been an accident? Is Tommy all right?"

Reassured that his sixteen-year-old son was not a traffic fatality, he seemed at a loss.

"It's about Shirley Knapp," Captain Heyer explained.

"At this hour?"

Without elaboration, Heyer told him what had occurred at National Airport. Macnamara had been leading them toward the living room but these few words were enough to deflect him.

"We'd better use my study . . . Don't worry, Kate," he called to his wife. "Tommy's all right. Something else has come up."

Despite this husbandly reassurance, he was grave-faced as he offered chairs. "Christ, and I thought we were in a mess before!" He smiled bitterly. "I suppose when Shirley Knapp gets herself murdered, the police think of three names right off the bat—me and Praeger and Adelman."

"We'll be talking to a lot of people," said Heyer stolidly.

"Sure. But guess which ones will get the headlines?" He closed his eyes briefly before continuing: "Well, you didn't come here just to give me the good news. What can I do for you?"

Although this witness sounded more responsive than John Carrington, Rudolph Heyer did not forget that he was dealing with a U. S. Congressman. He edged into his subject.

"Did you know that Mrs. Knapp was coming back to Washington today?"

"No, I assumed she was stuck in that hospital." Macnamara was thoughtful. "As a matter of fact, the Ad Hoc Committee did, too. I was talking to Ben Safford this afternoon and he told me that Carrington was lined up to testify on Monday. The committee wouldn't settle for Carrington if it could get Shirley Knapp."

Heyer saw a perfect opening. "What time was that, when you were talking to Safford?"

Macnamara had been thinking along different lines. He was momentarily taken aback, but he answered readily enough. "That must have been about three o'clock, because I was at the Shoreham by three-thirty. There was a convention over there and I was on the platform. Is that what you want to know?"

"It'd be a help if you went on."

Macnamara interpreted this liberally. "There was a big crowd there from Concord—that's my district. I went back to a party they were throwing at the Mayflower and glad-handed for about an hour. Then somewhere around six, I decided to call it a day. I came straight home and I've been right here ever since."

This would at least get the police started, Heyer thought.

"Thank you for being co-operative," he said formally.

Co-operative was not the word Heyer would have used to describe Herbert Adelman.

"No," said the young congressman when asked if he had known anything about Shirley Knapp's return to Washington.

"You thought she was still in the hospital in Ohio?" Heyer prodded.

"Yes."

Adelman was not volunteering a thing. He had jerked open the door of his room at the Carlton only after persistent knocking, and had stood, framed in the doorway, forbiddingly silent. His only reaction to news of Shirley Knapp's murder had been to march back to his chair and put down the half-eaten sandwich in his hand. When he finally turned to face the policemen, it was not to express unguarded emotion.

"What time did it happen?" he had demanded.

Heyer had taken Shirley Knapp's 4:38 arrival as a good place to begin. But so far he had flushed only the bare minimum. With Congressman Adelman, he decided, preliminaries were a waste of time.

"Would you mind telling me how you spent the afternoon?" he asked baldly.

For a moment, it seemed as if Adelman might refuse. He was, however, composing an answer.

"I was up on the Hill until everyone started going home. Then I left my office and came back here to work. That's what I was doing when you came."

Fine, said Heyer to himself. No details, no times, no witnesses. "Can you be a little more specific?" he asked.

"I don't see how," said Adelman evenly.

Heyer indicated the tray with the empty beer bottle and the sandwich. "Room service send that up?"

Adelman nodded and contributed his first fact. It was no help at all. Room service had arrived at ten o'clock.

A hasty late-night snack fit the picture nicely, Heyer thought as he examined his surroundings. Adelman himself was in shirt sleeves. Documents were scattered around his chair; on the table beside him, a pair of horn-rims rested on a yellow pad covered with jottings. The ashtray was overflowing.

It looked convincing, but Captain Heyer had a good memory. "We tried calling you a while back, Mr. Congressman. There wasn't any answer."

Adelman flinched. "I told the desk I wasn't taking any calls." Grudgingly, he added: "You can ask them."

Captain Heyer had a lot more than that to ask the desk.

"You want to know where I was? Perhaps it will interest you to learn, Captain, that Mrs. Praeger and I have just been dining with the Speaker of the House."

Warren Praeger had not been pleased to find the police waiting at his 16th Street apartment, and even less pleased to learn why they were there. While Mrs. Praeger exclaimed with horror, he drew himself up to his full five-feet-five and reminded Heyer of his political clout.

Details of any kind are welcome to policemen.

"I suppose there were a lot of people there," Heyer suggested.

"Only close friends of the Speaker," said Praeger, radiating satisfaction.

Heyer decided that this would give him plenty of witnesses. Time was the other factor. "And when did this dinner begin?"

Praeger answered by appealing to his wife. "Let's see . . . the invitation was for six. I'd say we were right on time, wouldn't you, Mildred?"

Placidly Mrs. Praeger agreed. "Yes, dear." She beamed at Captain Heyer. "I always think it's so nice if your hostess doesn't have to worry about whether you're coming."

"Yes, ma'am," he said, before reverting to her husband. "And what about the period before dinner, Mr. Congressman? Say, from four-thirty on?"

Praeger swelled with indignation. "I will not tolerate this. There is no reason why I should be singled out—"

"Now, Warren," Mrs. Praeger murmured. "Don't get on your high horse. Captain Heyer, here, is just doing his job."

This gentle intervention had its effect.

"I realize that, Mildred. However, I still regard this as unjustifiable intrusion . . ." But when she put a plump hand on his elbow, he capitulated. "Oh well, then . . . You wanted to know what I was doing before dinner? I was at my desk until five. Then I had an appointment with Otto Buchak. We talked for about twenty-five minutes. After that I came straight home to pick up Mildred."

"Thank you," said Heyer while Mrs. Praeger smiled approvingly. Unfortunately the harmony was short-lived. "And did you have any idea that Mrs. Knapp was flying into Washington today?"

"I most certainly did not," said Praeger resoundingly. "And, as she was supposed to be too unwell to travel, I can see no reason why she would have taken anybody into her confidence."

Captain Heyer could think of one very good reason.

CHAPTER 6

Shirley Knapp's murder hit Washington like an earthquake. The first jolt reached Ben Safford as he left the annual dinner meeting of the Midwest Highway Users. An ambush lay waiting for him just outside the Assembly Room.

"Whoa!" he answered the press. "I don't know what you're talking about—"

Breathlessly, someone relayed the terse police announcement that had already interrupted prime-time programs, then stabbed a microphone toward him.

Ben did not hesitate. Before Channel 4 could ask, he said: "I am shocked by this news. And that's all I can say right now."

As he spoke, he tucked his head down and made for the exit despite a trail of protests. Nobody was satisfied with a conventional response to murder, not when there was a hospital cross-examination and the Ad Hoc Committee to talk about. But, Ben thought as he hailed a taxi on 14th Street, there is a time and place for everything. The hours and days ahead were going to provide opportunity enough to analyze the implications of Shirley Knapp's death.

The phone on his desk was jangling when he got home to the Carlton.

"Oh no, you don't," he said, proceeding directly to bed.

But the aftermath was not as bad as he expected. For once, Capitol Hill did not resound with wagging tongues. Amidst shaking heads and somber faces, Val Oakes spoke for many: "Bad business," he summed up, after he and Ben told the networks that they still had no extended comment.

Only the NPA went beyond conventional expressions of horror. Mrs. Knapp had been a dedicated employee whose loss would be long felt. As for unfortunate suggestions about the NPA safe, it could now be revealed that the petty cash fund had been made whole with Mrs. Knapp's personal check for $1,982.00. The spokesman was confident that other innuendoes would prove equally groundless.

"It's almost as if people were holding their breath," said Madge that afternoon, reporting the uneasy stillness along the grapevine.

"They're waiting for the ax to fall," said Ben realistically. "Any minute now, all hell is going to break loose around here . . ."

But the first rumblings did not come from the Speaker, from Otto Buchak, or even Congressmen Macnamara, Adelman, or Praeger.

"Your sister Janet told me to get in touch with you, once I got to Washington," said Charlie Knapp laconically enough to make Madge, listening on the extension, arch her eyebrows.

Ben decided to skip condolences. "Whatever I can do to help," he offered.

"We-ell," said Knapp undecidedly. "I've got to go downtown and talk to the police . . ."

"I'll meet you," Ben told him. He did not know, any more than Knapp did, whether an escort would help. He did know what Janet would think.

In any event, Knapp seemed glad to see him arrive outside headquarters.

"I got a call from Shirley's lawyer and grabbed the first plane this morning," he said in reply to Ben's query. "I went straight out to Shirl's house in Chevy Chase. Then this guy Heyer said he'd like to talk to me."

With a philosophic shrug, he mounted the steps. Knapp was still casual, still in sports shirt and slacks. If there was a new tension around his mouth, Ben did not think it was because of the police.

"It's just like I told the cops in Newburg when they turned up last night," Knapp said once introductions were completed.

Warily, Captain Heyer glanced at Charlie Knapp's congressman. "We know," he said neutrally. "We'd just appreciate your running over it for us, Mr. Knapp."

Ben was tempted to explain that Charlie was not complaining or trying to pull strings. But since the policeman was not apologizing either, he decided to sit tight.

"Okay," Knapp said indifferently. "Shirley called me from the hospital about noon. Said she wanted her suitcase because she was leaving."

"Did she say why?" Heyer asked.

"She didn't say—and I didn't ask," said Charlie. "When I got there, it turned out she was taking the afternoon plane so I told her I'd give her a lift out to the airport. That left us with over an hour to kill, so we stopped to eat at the Wagon Wheel."

What about conversation at lunch?

"Shirley and I didn't have a helluva lot we wanted to talk about."

This picture of two people sharing prolonged silences was vivid, but not helpful.

"Did she say anything about Washington?" Heyer persisted.

"No, but she called someone here. She cleaned me out of change for the pay phone."

This was one point the police in Newburg had not uncovered.

"Do you know who she called?" Heyer asked quickly.

"No."

It was like pulling teeth for both of them.

"Then I took her to the plane," Charlie concluded.

Here was where Captain Heyer lost interest in Charlie Knapp, although he conscientiously took him through the rest of his day. The result came as a relief to Ben Safford. Knapp had carried Shirley's suitcase to the gate, then returned to Newburg to oversee his work crew until quitting time. He had spent the evening with his bowling league.

"Charlie," Ben said, deciding that Captain Heyer could use a hand, "did you get any idea of what Shirley was up to? Even if she didn't say anything, sometimes people don't have to—"

Belatedly, he realized that he might be touching a sore spot. How well did Charlie Knapp know Shirley? Their marriage, after all, had been a long time ago.

"I can't tell you a damned thing," said Knapp without constraint. "Except that Shirley was after somebody's scalp. I recognized that look!"

The wounds, Ben saw, had healed.

"Carrington admits Mrs. Knapp was coming to talk things over with him," Heyer said, discreetly appraising Ben. "But if she got in touch with anybody else, they're keeping quiet about it. Like your daughter, Mr. Knapp." He paused invitingly, then went on: "Or Congressmen Adelman, Praeger, or Macnamara."

Here it comes, thought Ben, bracing himself as Captain Heyer looked directly at him.

"Now, you've been going into this bribe, haven't you, Mr. Safford?"

"And making no progress," Ben assured him. "What we've got is proof that Mrs. Knapp said she gave a congressman fifty thousand dollars. We don't know if she really did, we don't know if she was authorized by Carrington—"

Captain Heyer cut in: "I was thinking about the other end. You know more about congressmen than I do . . ."

Pretending to misunderstand would be a waste of time. "We haven't questioned the congressmen yet," Ben said. "And so there's nothing I can tell you, that isn't already common knowledge."

Sounding disheartened, Heyer indicated acceptance. "I guess we're going to have to do it the hard way. Of course, if you do turn anything up . . . ?"

With certain reservations, Ben pledged co-operation and joined Charlie in leaving.

"Well, that wasn't so bad," he said, relaxing prematurely.

"Say, Ben," said Knapp, halting at the cab rank, "have you ever heard of this Burlington and Avery?"

Almost everybody in Washington had heard of this distinguished law firm, Ben replied.

"Not a bunch of ambulance chasers, huh?"

"No."

Charlie still delayed. "I don't suppose you've got any more time to spare?"

For some reason, he was more worried about a visit to these lawyers than he had been about a visit to the police. Even without directives from Janet and Madge, Ben could recognize a duty looming ahead.

They were halfway down Connecticut Avenue before Charlie dropped a clue. "I told Alison to meet me there," he offered. "She's old enough to know where she stands."

Ben chose his words with care. "Er . . . you and Alison getting along all right?"

"I suppose so." Charlie bit down hard but his feelings were too much for him. "The trouble with Shirley," he erupted, "was that she always had to do everything with such a goddammed bang."

Ben was not going to ask what this meant. But once launched, Charlie could not stop.

"You know, we were together for seven years. I don't say it was roses all the way, but still you get into habits. And a fat lot of good that does with Shirl! One day you're a father, the next day you come home to an empty house. Then fourteen years go by, you get used to not having a wife and kids—then boom! You're head of a family again."

Belatedly Ben realized the full scope of Charlie's problems. First, the past had knocked on his door and demanded refuge. Then there had been the dramatics with the hospital. And, it now developed, Charlie was not out of the woods yet.

Some encouragement was in order. "Did you drop everything to come here and take care of the kids? That must be pretty rough."

"Somebody's got to do it," Charlie muttered. "And it looks like I'm elected."

The taxi had managed to fight its way to the Randolph Building. They had traded the seedy interior of Police Headquarters for the elegant décor of Mr. Jason Freedburg's office. But in other ways the atmosphere had gone downhill.

Alison was already there. For some reason Ben had expected a transformation in her. So much had happened since he last saw her—the death of a mother, the arrival of a strange father, the descent of the police. With a start Ben realized that only three days had gone by. It was not surprising that Alison had not aged. And the resemblance was emphasized by the fact that she was treating the offices of Burlington & Avery the same way she treated Capitol Hill.

Unfortunately she and Mr. Freedburg had not hit it off. To be fair, Ben decided this might not be Alison's fault. Mr. Freedburg seemed to disapprove of his clients, their affairs, and their relatives.

"I have already told Miss Knapp that it is her father who is primarily concerned with my late client's will," he informed the newcomers.

Charlie was back in form. "Go on," he said briefly.

But Mr. Freedburg had barely begun his list of grievances. "I urged Mrs. Knapp to regularize her situation. If she was not prepared to undertake a divorce, we could have arranged a legal separation. But she would not be guided by me."

For the first time since his arrival in Washington, Charlie was amused. "I'll bet," he said.

While Freedburg recovered, Ben intervened. "So the two of you just let things drift?" he inquired conversationally.

It was probably the formality of Burlington & Avery that encouraged a Ben-and-Charlie, two plain guys from Ohio, tone. But Ben was also genuinely curious.

Charlie now had both hands in his pockets and was examining the potted plants reflectively. "Not worth the trouble doing anything," he replied absently.

There was an outraged inhalation from Freedburg, who now made another attempt to control the meeting. "Mrs. Knapp's will was drawn up several years ago. I strongly urged her to review its major provisions—"

"But she didn't," Charlie finished for him.

This earned him a glare. "Perhaps you will allow me to give you the broad outlines first," Freedburg said icily.

First came repayment of a loan of $6,342—"to be paid immediately to Charles S. Knapp."

Mr. Freedburg was interrupted.

"What's that for?" Alison demanded. "Why were you lending Mother money?"

Charlie's level gaze rested on his daughter. He took his time about answering.

"You could call it a loan," he said with a wry quirk of his lips.

"That was what Shirl emptied from our savings account when she walked out on me."

Alison was stupefied. "Six thousand dollars!" she echoed.

"I will proceed," declared Freedburg, rising above petty cash.

There was not much more. Shirley Knapp had left the rest of her estate in trust for her daughter Alison and her son William. Named as guardian, trustee, and sole executor was—Charles S. Knapp.

". . . here described as a devoted husband."

Freedburg was asking for a punch in the nose. He might even have gotten it if Alison had not immediately swung into action.

"All that was written years ago," she announced. "Before I was grown up. That business about trustees and guardians doesn't apply to me any more. Now Billy," she conceded, "he may still need a guardian."

"Billy's fourteen," Charlie told the room.

"Anyway," Alison retorted, "I don't see why you should be his guardian. Why, you don't even know him."

Freedburg had been itching to air his expertise. "Even if Mr. Knapp has not seen his son since infancy, he is still his father in the eyes of the law."

"Never saw him before today," Charlie corrected. "Shirl was pregnant when she lit out. As a matter of fact, he was the first thing I asked about when she turned up again."

"You asked about Billy?" Alison bridled. "Why him?"

"I never knew if it was a boy or a girl."

The resulting silence made it easy for the attorney to return to his theme. "And now we come to the estate itself." He waited for the sensations usually evoked by this phrase. But today was proving to be an exception all along the line. Freedburg decided these people did not know the right questions to ask. So, with considerable relish, he told them that the estate would be much smaller than they anticipated. There was a substantial mortgage on the property in Chevy Chase. The investment portfolio was not large. Other assets would not bring much.

"Mrs. Knapp, although earning a large income, did not accumulate," he ended sternly.

Charlie was scratching his chin and looking back at his youth. "Shirl always was a spender," he said reminiscently.

Alison seized on this. "I don't see how you can say that. You don't know anything about it. Anyway, we just lived normally."

Charlie blinked, but kept the peace.

Freedburg could see that his news had been a shock. He hastened to add a reassuring note. "However, with proper disposition of the assets and reasonable care of the proceeds, a college education for both children will be ensured. And possibly something beyond."

Alison did not like what she heard. "What do you mean, disposition of the assets?"

Mr. Freedburg was happy to instruct. "After the property in Maryland has been sold—"

"But we live in that house!"

"I am afraid that will no longer be feasible."

Alison glowered at him for a moment, then turned to Charlie who simply nodded.

"All right," she said. "If you're going to sell the house, then half the money is mine. I'll get an apartment for myself. It will be better that way, anyhow."

Freedburg raised a hand. "Miss Knapp! I'm afraid you don't understand. Your father is your trustee until you are twenty-one. Any disbursements beyond income will have to be very carefully scrutinized."

"Twenty-one! But that's not for two years!"

"Nevertheless your father is responsible for you until then."

"You mean I have to ask him whether I can do things? But that's silly. I'm nineteen." Her voice was rising. "And I'm exceptionally mature."

Two of the adults had enough sense to keep quiet. Mr. Freedburg, however, had been holding himself in too long.

"I suppose you regard your recent performance as mature. Let me tell you, Miss Knapp, that your mother would probably be alive today if you had not publicized her affairs. It gives me no pleasure to say this, but I have to—"

"No, you don't," Charlie said quietly.

Fleetingly, Ben thought that dislike of Freedburg might unite the Knapp family. But Alison, white-faced, had jumped to her feet and was choking over her words.

"You think I have to listen to you and do what you want.

But I don't have to stay here. There are lots of other things I can do." She was now moving rapidly. "And you'll be sorry. All of you."

The first dry sob escaped her just before she slammed the door.

CHAPTER 7

Ben Safford was not the only congressman pitchforked into an uncomfortable encounter by Shirley Knapp's murder. For instance, there was Representative Milton Seeburg (D-N.Y.), who had served in the House even longer than Ben. Trouble had stormed right into his office, in the person of Herb Adelman who was prowling the room like a caged beast.

"Sure, I sympathize," said Seeburg wearily. "But what good is sympathy?"

"That's right," Adelman retorted.

Seeburg ignored the remark. "You can't expect miracles from the committee. Not when the police have barely started their job."

"And where does that leave me?" Adelman, his teeth clenched, ground out the words. "The police have a job, the committee has a job, even the papers have a job. And none of them gives a good goddam about my election next November—" He broke off.

Seeburg shrugged eloquently. "That's life."

It was doubtful if Adelman heard him. "But I might get them working for me," he murmured, as if responding to an inner voice. "Other people have done it. You just can't tell . . ."

"I don't know what you're talking about," Seeburg interjected.

Whatever Adelman's uncertainties, he had resolved them. "I've got an idea, Milt. Listen to this, and see how it grabs you."

Five minutes later, Seeburg was looking at his young colleague with wary respect. "Thirty years ago this would have finished you," he warned.

"We're talking about today, not thirty years ago," was the uncompromising reply.

Seeburg nodded. "Nowadays you can't tell." But he was willing to accept the odds. "I don't say it's a sure thing. But at least it will put you front and center."

Freshmen congressmen do not often call press conferences, for one good reason. They would end up addressing an empty room. Herbert Adelman, however, did not have to worry. In the first place, he was a suspect in the Shirley Knapp case and the press was not finding it easy to buttonhole the others.

In the second place, every reporter covering the Hill kept an ear to the ground for tremors from the office of Congressman Milton Seeburg. And hints from that quarter had been flowing for over twenty-four hours.

Seeburg himself called a Washington bureau chief. "We've been meaning to get together for lunch, Scotty," he said. "What do you say to tomorrow—but no, that won't give us enough time. You'll be covering Adelman at two o'clock. How about the day after tomorrow?"

His administrative assistant had a hot tip for a network anchorman. "It'll be worth your while to attend Adelman's conference."

At lower levels, the same game was played. Congressman Seeburg's secretary was a gray-haired woman of fifty with enough political savvy to run Congress by herself.

"What a day!" she confided to the right people. "The telephone has been ringing all morning about Mr. Adelman's press conference. I guess everybody will be there."

After this treatment, everybody was. Herb Adelman had gotten his standing-room-only crowd; the performance was up to him.

When a presidential candidate or a Senate Majority Leader meets the press, he strides in flanked by aides, while clerks circulate copies of his statement.

Adelman chose a different approach. He arrived, almost on time, accompanied only by his wife. On the threshold, they momentarily recoiled from the bedlam within, before moving forward to the microphones. There was no manuscript, no sheaf of notes. Herb Adelman was going to speak from the heart.

He made two false starts. Then he cleared his throat and squared his shoulders.

"Ladies and gentlemen, it is time that someone told the truth about the Shirley Knapp accusations and the vote on Section C. If you will bear with me, I would like to review some events that took place eighteen months ago."

He began with the history of the Industrial Pollution Bill. Shortly after his assignment to the Gellert Subcommittee, he was approached by Mrs. Shirley Knapp.

"It was the first of many contacts," he said, "and, for a long time, I did not realize what was going on. During our early meetings, Mrs. Knapp stayed well within proper limits. She presented the NPA case, and she did it very well. I was already dubious about including the private power industry."

The room was silent except for the scrabbling of pencils. By now the press corps could not tell what was coming next—and this *is* unusual in Washington.

"Then, very gradually, Mrs. Knapp changed her tactics. I was attending a dinner by myself, and she commented on the absence of my wife. From there one thing led to another. She was very knowledgeable about the costs of a congressman who really tries to serve his district. Expenses are high, and something has to give. In my case, it was the second home that would make it possible for my wife and our son David to share my life in Washington with me. I should have recognized the danger of discussing such subjects with Mrs. Knapp. My eyes were not opened until later, when she told me that she had been considering my problems and suggested that she could help. I then saw where she was heading and immediately broke off the conversation. But she did not give up easily. She called my office, she sent me invitations to NPA functions, she tried to single me out at parties. I avoided all her attempts to reopen our talks."

He pulled out a handkerchief and mopped his brow.

"Christ!" muttered an AP man. "Do you mean he got us down here for this? To say he was a good little boy who refused to eat the apple?"

"That was the last time I spoke with Mrs. Knapp—until the day of her death," Adelman said firmly.

Sensation!

He surveyed the room grimly, waiting for the noise to subside.

"She called me from National Airport at five o'clock Friday afternoon. I want to tell you what she said to me."

Several men were poised half out of their seats, ready to break for the phones. But the time of this conference had been carefully scheduled. The six o'clock news would show it on television. So would the eleven o'clock roundup. Herb Adelman was bypassing the evening newspapers and taking his story directly into the nation's living rooms.

"She sounded desperate. She said she was offering me a deal for my own good. Four people were on the spot—three congressmen and herself. We were all going to have to hang together if we wanted to survive. She wanted the three of us to testify that she had never said or done anything which could be construed as the overture to a bribe. And then she started threatening. If Shirley Knapp went down, she would take the rest of us with her. Every voter in the country would think all three of us had been on the NPA payroll. If I wanted to prevent this, I'd have to take her orders. That's the choice she gave me." His face darkened. "I told her to go to hell and I hung up. My next information about Shirley Knapp was when they told me that someone had gone out to the airport and murdered her."

"Beautiful!" murmured a veteran reporter. "I don't know whether it's good politics, but it's great staging."

Meanwhile Adelman had taken a sip of water and was once again facing the cameras.

"This is the first time I have revealed these details. Making this decision was not easy. Yesterday I asked my wife to come to Washington and help me with her counsel. This is her concern as well as mine because it may well mean the end of our present life. And she agreed with me that the American people have a right to know what is going on inside their government. There are those who advised against taking this action. But I believe my constituents should know not only how I have acted, but how I have been treated. Unless American voters can take with them to the polls certain basic information about the pressures that bear on their elected representatives, they are deprived of the knowledge they need in making their choice. I have nothing with which to reproach myself. I have never taken a penny from Shirley Knapp. My actions have never been dictated by the NPA or any other pressure group. Throughout my term I have served the interests of the people of my district to the best of my ability. And, God willing, I will do so again."

Irene Adelman had come to her husband's side when he first mentioned her. Throughout the latter part of his speech she had clasped his elbow. Now, as his voice died away, they stood shoulder to shoulder, looking very young and vulnerable. It was a moment before the room erupted with questions.

"Did Shirley Knapp say anything about fifty thousand dollars?"

"What did you feel like when you hung up on her? Did you feel like shooting her?"

And Mrs. Adelman came in for her share.

"Aren't you proud to be part of your husband's decision, Mrs. Adelman?"

"Would you answer a few questions about the difficulties of running a home in New York while your husband works in Washington?"

She had the easier task of the two. Flustered and stammering, Irene Adelman repeated shyly that she was proud of her husband. And the Adelmans both agreed that the moral rewards of a life of service compensated for the sacrifices they were making.

Adelman had said what he wanted to say. But one piece of housekeeping remained.

"What about the police?" yelled an avid voice. "Do they know anything about all this?"

"I'm on my way to tell them now." Adelman flashed a cocky grin. "Before they come and get me."

"It's nice of you to remember us," Heyer said sarcastically.

Adelman refused to be baited. "You caught me off guard the other night, when you told me about Shirley Knapp's murder," he said doggedly. "Hell, I was still worrying about what she was going to do to me. But as soon as it all sank in, I decided I'd better lay everything out on the table for you."

Captain Heyer was not overawed by junior congressmen.

"Only stopping off to take the whole country into your confidence first," he observed. "You're playing politics while we've got a murder on our hands."

This earned him a level glance from intense dark eyes. "This whole Shirley Knapp business has been politics from the word go, and it still is. You know that as well as I do," Adelman retorted.

Heyer could be stubborn, too. "Maybe that's the way you look at it, but I'm out to catch a killer."

"Great! I'm all for it. But I'm not apologizing for anything. Your job is to catch killers without wrecking a lot of innocent lives."

"Okay." Heyer made a gesture of dismissal. "For openers, let's start with this phone call from National. You claim she wanted all three of you to swear that she never even hinted about a bribe."

"That's right."

"Then she was going to contact the other two? Is that what you mean?" Heyer demanded.

Adelman was totally expressionless. "I have no idea what she was going to do."

"Did she say anything about Macnamara or Praeger?"

"No."

"And you didn't ask?"

"No, I got off the phone right away. I had a lot of heavy thinking to do."

Captain Heyer had drawn his own conclusion. "Logically, she should have put the pressure on the others, also."

The same thought had occurred to Warren Praeger.

"Who the hell would expect Adelman to pull something like this?" he bleated.

On the other end of the line, Dick Macnamara was more detached. "Well, it doesn't seem to be doing him any harm, does it?"

The six o'clock news had featured not only an extended clip of Congressman Herbert Adelman, but a short interview with his wife as well. Irene had been unexpectedly appealing.

"It may not have done him any harm, but it's done us plenty," Praeger snapped. "You heard him insinuate that Shirley telephoned us, too. She probably told him so. That's why he didn't mind sticking his neck out."

"He didn't actually say that Shirley called you and me," Macnamara objected sharply.

"All right, all right. But even so, look where he's left us. Dick, there's nothing for us to do but follow his lead."

"I'll be damned if I dance to his tune—" Macnamara began.

"I don't like it any more than you do. But my God,"—Praeger was pleading now—"they're not going to let us alone. And if we have to see the police, I say we should talk to them under circumstances where we have some control."

Macnamara digested this in silence. He did not have to be told that Warren Praeger wanted as many support factors as possible when he confronted the police. What's more, there might be advantages for Richard Macnamara in such an arrangement.

"You may be right," he said finally. "But let's get one thing straight. Just how much are you planning to confide in this Captain Heyer?"

"I'll tell him about Shirley's call at five o'clock," Praeger said pompously. "That may help him with times or something like that . . ."

This was not what Macnamara meant.

"And your earlier dealings with Mrs. Knapp?" he challenged.

There was an unhappy pause. Then: "I shall state she made several attempts to broach the subject of Section C, and that I invariably rebuffed her." Praeger was catching his second wind. "I see no reason to burden the police with details which can be of no conceivable use to them."

"I'll bet you don't," Macnamara said—to himself.

CHAPTER 8

Warren Praeger asked for support factors, and he got more than he bargained for. The Speaker not only set up a meeting in the Rayburn Building with Captain Heyer, he dispatched a team of observers.

Congressmen Benton Safford and Eugene Valingham Oakes were there to remind everybody that the House of Representatives was not forgetting its own investigation. When they appeared, Praeger blanched, Macnamara smiled wryly and Captain Heyer frowned.

Nevertheless, Praeger took the plunge. He had, he was now ready to admit, received a phone call from Shirley Knapp at a little after five o'clock, last Friday.

"She was crazy! You should have heard the things she said," he wound up. "She was totally out of control. It was . . . intolerable."

Captain Heyer made it as easy as possible for Macnamara. "Is that how you felt about it, Congressman?" he inquired.

Macnamara grimaced. "I didn't enjoy it," he said constrainedly.

"That's not what I meant. Do you agree she was out of control?"

"You couldn't really describe our conversation as coherent." Macnamara ran a hand through his hair as he searched for words. "All that business of Herb's about Shirley Knapp wanting to take everybody down with her was true enough. She was raving, but I was raving myself. I wasn't only mad, I was surprised. You know," he said, glancing toward Ben and Val, "that scheme of hers about the four of us swearing she had never stepped over the mark? It never would have worked, and she should have known it. If you ask me, she had cut her own throat with that memo, and it was driving her wild."

Macnamara's frankness had its effect. "I expect that was because of Carrington," Praeger said knowingly.

"Carrington?" Heyer asked. "Adelman didn't mention him."

Praeger looked as if he regretted speaking, but Macnamara would not let him retreat. "Go on, Warren. There's no point backing off now."

Uneasily, Praeger continued: "She told me she had to give Carrington something concrete."

"In other words, the NPA was getting ready to throw her to the wolves," Macnamara concluded.

Heyer was not interested in what Macnamara thought. "Is that what she told you?"

"Not outright. But she was boiling over, and I got the distinct impression that she'd been on the receiving end of an ultimatum herself."

Ben did not blame Heyer for losing patience.

"So what it comes down to is that Mrs. Knapp called each of you from National," the policeman said heavily. "After that, you all went on as if nothing had happened."

There was an immediate disclaimer.

"Not exactly."

Captain Heyer leaned toward Dick Macnamara. "Like to make some more changes in your statement?" he asked softly.

"No, I wouldn't! But if nothing had happened, I'd have stayed in the office. Instead, I headed home. I didn't want that madwoman to reach me again."

Ben realized that he and Oakes were nodding comprehension. They could follow Macnamara's reasoning right down to the wire. Mrs. Knapp would probably hesitate to descend on a crowded domestic scene. And, if worse came to worst, in Bethesda there would be witnesses.

"And you, Congressman Praeger? After you rejected Shirley Knapp's demands, did you let her call influence your behavior?"

"I've already told you that I spent most of the evening at a party with my wife."

But the Washington Police Force had been busy.

"Yes, sir. We have since learned that you arrived late."

Coloring slightly, Praeger said: "I must have forgotten to mention it. The pressure of work required me to finish a few tasks before joining my wife."

"What were those tasks?"

Praeger fell back on offended dignity. "I fail to see what difference that makes."

"Mr. Praeger, we're talking about the period during which Mrs. Knapp was murdered," Heyer was emphatic. "You don't want me to think you used that hour to rush out to the airport and—"

"No!" Praeger roared. "You have no right to make that kind of assumption. I was in my study at home!"

"Doing what?" the captain pressed. "You had planned to leave with your wife, hadn't you? Was it Shirley Knapp who made you stay home?"

"All right, it was."

"What were you doing?"

Praeger, looking hunted, met Val Oakes's sleepy gaze of speculation. Better men than he had been unnerved by that experience. With visible effort, he jerked his eyes away.

"If you must know, I was thinking," he said defiantly to Heyer.

"I see."

"No, you don't! But you ought to be able to. This woman calls me out of the blue. Then she makes these preposterous threats. I wanted to be by myself. Maybe there was something I should be doing."

Captain Heyer, Ben could see, suspected something had been left unsaid. Otherwise, why was Praeger so defensive? After all, Adelman had admitted putting off his trip to New York. Macnamara had fled behind the barrier of his family.

The sticking point for them had been the phone call, not their reaction to it. But, if the police were at a loss to explain Warren Praeger's evasiveness, Val Oakes was not.

"It's as plain as the nose on your face, Elsie," he was expounding some hours later. "Old Warren dug his heels in, and wouldn't tell the police a thing. But we all know what he did after he heard from Shirley Knapp. He skedaddled home to burn every piece of paper he ever got from her."

71

No one entered into the spirit of extracurricular relaxation more than Mrs. Hollenbach. But even over late-afternoon Bourbon in Val's office she had been known to draw the line.

"Now, don't look at me that way, Elsie," said Val, who registered more than a lot of people gave him credit for. "What would you do, if you were in his predicament?"

Oakes's large tolerance had misled him. Urging Elsie to visualize herself in Warren Praeger's shoes was going too far. Fortunately, Tony Martinelli diverted everybody from this collision course.

"When you said predicament," he commented sagely, "you said a mouthful."

"Sure, Praeger's in a mess," said Ben, honoring the convention of not asking Tony direct questions. "But Macnamara and Adelman are, too."

"From what I hear," Tony replied sleekly, "Praeger's the one in real trouble."

What Tony heard, and whom he heard it from, was a source of endless speculation to his colleagues, including Mrs. Hollenbach.

"By real trouble," she said crisply, "I assume you are referring to his election next fall."

"What else?" demanded Tony, presenting the palms of his hands to heaven. "You don't think I'd know anything about bribes, do you, Elsie?"

Among Mrs. Hollenbach's many other abilities was the capacity to resist provocation. Biting down hard, she replied: "Of course, a scandal of this magnitude will hurt the chances of all three. But, on the whole, I would have thought Warren Praeger was in a better position than either Adelman or Macnamara."

By common consent, all eyes turned to L. Lamar Flecker, the ranking expert on safe seats. He smiled amiably and played straight man.

"Why sure, Tony," he said reflectively. "After all, Warren's been in for eight or nine terms. That gives him an edge over the other two. Adelman's in his first term and Macnamara's in his second. I don't say that Warren's set the world on fire while he's been up here, but he's voted the right way on the grain bills—and that's what they care about in Nebraska. Hell, while this poor kid from New York is scurrying around trying to make a name for himself so he can run against half a dozen people just like him, chances are Warren will be unopposed—"

A sibilant hiss told everybody that Tony had got just what he wanted. "That's it." He lowered his voice. "They tell me that some red-hot local has been busy. Praeger's been unopposed for the last five or six times out, but now he's facing a real threat."

He got respectful attention from four people who knew all there is to know about real threats.

"And," Tony went on with husky authority, "the way I hear it, Praeger hasn't kept in with the local organization. And Foley—that's the guy who's running against him—has already made big inroads. Long before Shirley Knapp's memo, Warren Praeger was in hot water."

Val bestirred himself to replenish Tony's drink. "Stands to reason," he observed, making a pass in Ben's direction with the bottle. "The truth is, Warren has been too damned lazy. He hasn't pulled his weight up here—and he hasn't mended fences at home."

But it was from Elsie that Tony got his real tribute, although an outsider might have mistaken her question for a partisan defense. "Surely no one," she asked obliquely, "can say that about Dick Macnamara. He has an excellent attendance record—"

Tony Martinelli was, as Ben always maintained, a thoroughgoing gentleman in his own way.

"I don't know a damned thing about Macnamara's prospects, Elsie," he said forthrightly. "I can always ask around."

By the time Elsie had fervently declined this offer, Lou Flecker's summary had lost some of its original thrust.

"Well, this Shirley Knapp uproar hits them all hard, but I guess it's going to hit poor old Warren hardest."

Even there, he did not find the consensus he expected.

"I do not see that," said Elsie. "Surely, the situation of a first-term congressman—and from New York City—is the most precarious. Say what you will, Praeger is known to the voters in his district. And Macnamara—leaving aside his record—is part and parcel of the community he represents. He has a real home there, and he and his family are still active in local affairs when Congress isn't in session. No, the most exposed one of these three is young Adelman. I admit that he's more flamboyant than the others, but he's still relatively unknown. His wife and baby may live in New York—"

"Brooklyn," said Tony sapiently.

"Brooklyn then," said Elsie, in no way discomposed. "But I'm sure they do not provide the same kind of identification."

This time, Tony spoke with malice aforethought. "Sure, Elsie," he said, smiling wickedly. "But one thing you've got to admit. From where I sit, it looks as if Warren Praeger was the guy who had the biggest need for a fast fifty thousand bucks."

An impeccable lady from the impeccable suburbs of San Francisco put Tony in his place.

"Tony," said Elsie without batting an eye, "have you ever known a politician, particularly a member of the House, who couldn't use a fast fifty thousand bucks—as you put it?"

While Tony reeled under this damaging counterpunch, Ben intervened.

"It all depends, doesn't it?" he began.

Val Oakes did not wait for clarification. "It always does, Ben," he rumbled. "It always does."

But Ben had not been aiming at a universal truth. "First of all," he said, "one of these three may well be arrested before November."

"Looked to me as if Heyer was just fishing this afternoon," Val argued.

Ben remembered the police checkout of Praeger's alibi. The real investigation was not taking place in the Rayburn Building, and God knew what it was turning up. "Anyway," he said firmly, "the murder's not in our bailiwick. But the bribe is. Until we get that cleared up, Adelman, Praeger, and Macnamara are all in trouble."

"And we are too," said Elsie, always one to face the unpalatable truth. Scandals in Congress, particularly when they break before elections, hurt every incumbent. There are too many clean brooms out on the hustings, ready to take over.

"Uh-huh," said Val lugubriously. "Any minute, people are going to start yelling that we shouldn't have postponed the hearings."

For a considerable interval, the gloom was uninterrupted. Under the best of circumstances, probing into allegations of wrongdoing by a fellow legislator is distasteful. Murder makes it worse.

"I can think of several steps to take before we decide when the hearings should resume," said Elsie, quaffing her drink manfully. "Even though we disagree on precisely when that should be."

Ben was there before her. "Yes," he said. "I'd like to talk with John Carrington off the record—now that he can put all the blame on Shirley."

Even in informal session, his committee backed him up.

"Good idea," said Val approvingly while Tony Martinelli studied the angles through the inch of amber remaining in his glass. Lou Flecker served as courthouse lawyer.

"Ben," he said with guileless blue eyes that deceived no one. "When you tackle Carrington, you tackle the NPA. Now, I don't like to see you marching into the lion's den all by yourself. Why don't you take someone along—oh, say Elsie."

Ben, like Elsie, appreciated the full subtlety of this.

So, the next morning did John Carrington.

"It's good of you to take the time to talk to me, Congressman," he said earnestly. "*And* Mrs. Hollenbach. Of course, now that Mrs. Knapp is gone . . ."

Some things, Ben was the first to admit, Elsie could handle better than he could.

"Mrs. Knapp's murder," she said, brushing aside euphemisms like crumbs, "is a police matter. The House of Representatives is still concerned with the bribe that the NPA is alleged to have given a congressman."

Carrington, to do him credit, did not wilt. "Yes, indeed," he said with unabated courtliness.

His assistant, however, had felt the brass knuckles. "The Ad Hoc Committee plans to resume the hearings?" he asked. "Can you tell us exactly when?"

"We will give everybody proper notice," said Ben formally. "At the moment, I can only say that we are in the process of deciding."

Before the assistant could muddy the waters, Carrington took over:

"It's inevitable," he said, as if timing were not critical. "After all, it's a very, very serious charge—suborning a member of Congress. I want you and Mrs. Hollenbach to know that, here at the NPA, we realize that—"

"Good," said Elsie, interrupting the flow.

"But," said Carrington, "I hope you understand our position. When an overzealous subordinate exceeds her authority . . ."

Shaking his head sadly, he broke off.

The Texas style takes time and Ben, for one, was willing to wait. Not so Elsie, who all but drummed her fingers. More abruptly than he intended, Carrington picked up his recital: "Naturally, we're going to try to find out if anyone in Houston knew what Mrs. Knapp was up to. But this is a bad week for me. You know, my boy is getting married."

He certainly had every right to assume they knew. Because Reed Carrington was marrying the daughter of the Vice-President of the United States. And, weather permitting, the ceremony would take place in the Rose Garden of the White House. By now the whole world had seen sketches of the bridesmaids' gowns, and the Republican National Committee had abandoned hope that the groom would break a leg.

"We weren't thinking of calling you until after the wedding," said Ben woodenly. One week, the Committee had agreed, was small price to pay to avoid a lot of static from 1600 Pennsylvania Avenue. "But after that, I think you'd better have your testimony ready."

Carrington was not smiling when he returned from seeing his guests off.

"Well, there it is!" he raged. "You heard Safford. I've got to come up with something."

His assistant was used to the Carrington temper. Barbara Underwood, on the other hand, was openly fascinated.

"Now that Shirley's dead," said Carrington, restlessly quartering the room as he thought aloud, "it's a whole new ball game."

"Now that Shirley's been murdered," said the assistant with a bravery that made Mrs. Underwood catch her breath.

Carrington shot him a piercing look. "You heard Mrs. Hollenbach," he said unpleasantly. "Whoever murdered Shirley—that's police business. Here we're concentrating on other things. Got that?"

When the assistant nodded, he went on: "The Safford committee is going to begin with Shirley. Then they're going to prove that the fifty thousand came from the NPA. But, what they're really after is the name of the man who took the bribe."

"Why don't we just tell them?" the assistant said.

"Because," Carrington replied, "we don't know the name."

The assistant knew better than to comment.

"If we could give Safford that name," Carrington mused aloud, "the heat would be off the NPA. That would give me something to trade with. But what do I have now? A pair of clean hands—and that's all."

Almost accidentally, he turned his attention to Mrs. Underwood. "Are you absolutely sure Shirley Knapp didn't drop any hints?"

She was wide-eyed. "Mr. Carrington, I truly didn't know she was bribing anyone. If I had, I'd have told you right away."

Carrington sighed. "I wasn't implying that you knew at the time, Barbara," he said apologetically. "But since then, you've been through the files. I just wondered if you'd found any leads there."

"But I was shredding papers, not reading them," she replied. Then, wrinkling her brow in thought, she added: "There was some material in Mrs. Knapp's logs. But I'm almost sure I didn't see anything that would help you."

With an effort, Carrington smiled warmly. "Well, we'd be real grateful if you do remember anything, Barbara. You can see how important it is to us."

"Oh, I'll do my best," she promised. "But Mrs. Knapp was so secretive."

"Yes," said Carrington, making it sound indulgent. "She was that. Well, I want you to know that we understand how hard all this has been for you. You've been a big help already."

The assistant waited until Mrs. Underwood left the room.

"Why waste time on that now?" he asked from long experience in watching secretaries melt under the Carrington treatment.

Carrington was still looking at the closed door.

"Pretending Shirley was the only one who knew who took that bribe is a lot of horseshit," he said in an ugly voice.

It was not the first time the assistant wondered what John Bowie Carrington meant.

CHAPTER 9

Until two weeks ago, Mrs. Barbara Underwood had been a typist and stenographer. Overnight she found herself conferring with Houston, stalling the press, and shredding files. Then John Carrington arrived, and she caught her first glimpse of behind-the-scenes politicking. Now she was determined never to go back to the typewriter again. By the next morning her plans were made.

"Are you finished with the paper yet, dear?" she asked across the breakfast table.

From behind a double sheet of newsprint, her husband said he was not. Commander Lyman Underwood, USN, approached the tasks of life with all due deliberation. At the moment he was carefully studying a letter to the editor about proposed changes in pay scales for servicemen.

His wife regarded him with affectionate exasperation. He was probably the only person in Washington, she thought, to skim blithely past the front page coverage of the Shirley Knapp scandal. Ly knew what he was interested in, and no layout man was changing his mind. At the moment the subject of concern was a salary hike. The Underwoods enjoyed the gracious things of life and were currently outrunning their income at an alarming rate.

"Is there anything in the news today?" she asked cunningly. He liked reading tidbits to her as if the *Post* were his personal informant.

But her tactics backfired.

"This will interest you," he said with simple assurance.

He read aloud the letter to the editor, then began an analysis of naval fringe benefits.

Barbara cast around for a diversion. The empty eggshells and crumbs on her husband's plate held out no hope. True, every now and then a disembodied hand groped for a cup, but Ly was capable of drinking any amount of coffee without interrupting his lecture.

"Boysenberry jam," she said, suddenly inspired. "I forgot your mother sent us a jar from California. Would you like some more toast with it?"

Ten minutes later, Commander Underwood disposed of the last crust and made a discovery.

"You've got the paper, Barbara," he said reproachfully.

"Why, so I do!" she agreed, handing it over without a murmur. With amusement she watched him refold the paper to page eight. Only once had Ly shown any interest in the events rocking her world—when the *Post* announced Mrs. Knapp's salary was fifty-three thousand dollars. To be honest, that had stopped her in her tracks, too.

Commander Underwood was still lost in calculations when he donned his jacket and cap, before joining his car pool to the Pentagon.

"Let's hope this pay raise goes through," he remarked. "It could work out to sixty dollars a month more."

"That would be wonderful, dear," said Barbara, even though seven hundred dollars a year suddenly seemed like an insignificant sum.

After he left, she dumped the dishes in the washer with less than her usual precision, made one brief call to the office, and was soon heading for the bus stop. But once there, she was overcome by a sense of occasion. This was no time for buses. Imperatively she flagged a taxi.

She could feel her heartbeat quickening as she opened the door. After six years of working in important Washington offices and recognizing famous Washington faces, she was finally going to say the magic words. Breathlessly she turned to the cabby.

"Capitol Hill," she directed firmly.

"Absolutely not!" said the receptionist, barring the way to Room 341.

"But you don't understand." Barbara Underwood was convinced there was some mistake. This was not the welcome she had foreseen. "I represent the NPA."

"Honey, that's why you're leaving."

Pink and determined, Barbara tried to argue the point. She was brutally cut off.

"And if you're not on your way by the time I count three, I'll call a House guard."

She was luckier at her next stop.

"I really don't know," the woman in the doorway said doubtfully.

"I'm Barbara Underwood, Mrs. Rodgers. We've talked on the phone several times."

The woman's face cleared.

"I remember you now, miss. You're Mrs. Knapp's secretary."

For once, Mrs. Underwood did not correct either error. "It's a shame to bother you," she said earnestly, "but it won't take me more than fifteen minutes. And I'll try not to get in your way."

The woman was still hesitating.

Barbara played her trump card. Drooping dejectedly, she became the living image of a downtrodden employee. Her voice grew plaintive. "I don't know what they'll say if I come back without it."

That did the trick. Clucking sympathetically, the woman stepped back. "And sending you all this way, too," she murmured.

Barbara was almost dancing as she stepped across the threshold.

Charlie Knapp was so angry he was stuttering.

"I'm not taking any more of this!" he fumed. "I don't care if this is Washington. That's not the way we do things where I come from."

Puzzled, Ben moved the phone a little farther from his ear. Charlie had managed to keep his cool so far. It was hard to imagine what had set him off.

"I still don't know what happened," he said patiently.

Charlie struggled for control. "I left the house for two hours. Just two goddam little hours."

"Yes?"

"There was nobody there but the housekeeper and Billy. He's got a cold and didn't go to school . . ."

Ben beat down a flicker of apprehension. Charlie would not be calling him, if anything serious had happened to the boy.

Charlie was continuing. "Seems some woman showed up and tanked right over Mrs. Rodgers. Said she was from the NPA and had to get a couple of files Shirley had brought home. That fool housekeeper left her alone in Shirl's study. Then Billy came downstairs."

It did not take the steady hardening of Charlie's voice to paint the picture for Ben.

"Go on," he said quietly.

"She couldn't find what she wanted at first. So she made Billy help her. He showed her where Shirl kept her log of calls from the house."

"Who was this woman?" Ben asked.

"Mrs. Rodgers says she was Shirley's secretary," Knapp replied. "That means she comes from Carrington, doesn't it?"

Ben countered with a question of his own. "Did she take anything?"

"An armload."

And what in the name of God was the NPA looking for now, Ben wondered. When last seen, John Carrington was trying to do a Pontius Pilate. This foraging raid, however, had a reminiscent smell to it. The aroma conjured up shredding machines and slush funds. Adelman, Praeger, and Macnamara might be the stars of the current drama, but the NPA was in the cast, too. It is a criminal offense to give a bribe, as well as to accept one. And as for murder . . .

"I don't like it," Charlie said heavily.

Ben could see why. Having strangers push their way past the help was bad enough. Having them involve unwary youngsters was worse.

But this intrusion disturbed him on other counts as well. An unknown quantity of material had disappeared from the Knapp home into the NPA's hands. Almost certainly it would re-emerge as ammunition of some kind at the hearings of the Ad Hoc Committee. As the man in charge of those hearings, Ben did not want any surprise packages. More immediate, however, was the problem of Charlie Knapp, who sounded ready to launch a guerrilla attack of his own.

"What are you going to do about it?" Ben asked, with a view to keeping the peace.

"Look, I know this Carrington thinks he's important. Hell, Alison tells me his kid's getting married in the White House. Well, that doesn't cut any ice with me. Either he learns to leave me and *my* kid alone, or he's not going to be in any shape to turn up for the doings."

That's all we need, thought Ben. With official Washington turning somersaults to make the great day a success, it would take only one black eye to bring the roof down.

"Charlie," he said urgently, "right now, I think your tangling with Carrington might be a mistake—"

"For who?" Charlie demanded.

Ben decided that the truth could use a little bending. "For everyone concerned." He hoped he sounded convincing. "Let me look into this, will you, before you do anything?"

"And what happens in the meantime? I suppose they'll be after Alison, next."

"God knows, I understand how you feel. But Charlie, we've got real complications on our plates. Going off half cocked won't help. At least, not until we know more about what Carrington's up to."

Charlie's natural good sense reasserted itself. "Okay," he said somberly. "Just as long as one thing's clear, Ben. The NPA comes out to the house again and . . ."

Ben did not have to see the clenched fist.

"I've got the message," he said. "And believe me, I'll pass it along."

Lyman Underwood cherished small routines. Every day, upon returning from the Bureau of Naval Personnel, he sailed into his kitchen where he painstakingly prepared two perfect martinis. Then he settled down to tell Barbara all about his triumphs and defeats since breakfast. To accommodate him, Barbara had learned how to half cook a gourmet meal, break off, then carry on. They were rarely interrupted.

Commander Underwood had just shaved his first curl of lemon peel when the phone rang. With knife poised, he muttered resentfully: "Who can that be?" before marching off to answer the call.

He was still aggrieved when he returned. "It's Carrington, from your office. I told him we were just about to eat, but he says he's got to talk to you."

By all rights, Barbara should have been on his side. Instead she downed her potholder with alacrity. "Just see that it doesn't boil over, will you, Ly?" she tossed back at him.

With a sense of injury, Ly Underwood returned to his shaker, not forgetting to keep a dutiful eye on the stove. He could hear nothing but occasional dulcet agreement from his wife. But whatever the result of the conversation, it had pleased her. She drifted back to the kitchen, stared at the skillet and her husband as if she had forgotten them both, then finally automatically lowered the flame. Still without a word, she picked up her drink and headed for the living room.

By the time her husband had joined her she was curled up in the corner of the sofa.

Ponderously he cleared his throat before beginning: "You remember I told you yesterday that Kidd wanted me to change my leave to July . . ."

But Barbara was staring into the distance. "That," she said dreamily, "was John Carrington."

The time had come to take a stand. "I don't like him calling you here after office hours."

"Oh, he apologized for that. He said it was an emergency. He's really a very considerate man."

Lyman Underwood snorted. "I don't see what's so wonderful about him."

"You would if you'd ever worked for Mrs. Shirley Knapp," Barbara replied with a sharpness quite unusual for her.

Underwood was momentarily baffled. Long ago he had settled it with himself that his wife worked to keep herself occupied. With no children and a husband away for long stretches of the day, what else could she do? In youthful periods of optimism, he had assumed that soon he would be an admiral, Barbara would be an admiral's lady and, in some mysterious fashion, she would have a full schedule. Whatever else they did, admirals' ladies did not get mixed up with murder suspects.

"What was the big emergency, anyway?" he asked skeptically.

Barbara was deliberately vague. "Oh, I have some material he wants. I told him I'd look through it tonight."

Lyman Underwood's routines were being shattered left and right. "But tonight's the second half of *Don Quixote*," he protested. The first half, both Underwoods agreed, had been television at its finest. "You said you were looking forward to it."

"You'll have to tell me all about it," she said absently. "There's no way of knowing how important these papers might be. John Carrington is terribly anxious about them. In fact, he wanted to—" She stopped short, then: "So I promised I'd look them over tonight and talk to him first thing in the morning."

But Ly Underwood had noticed the hesitation. "What did he want? You don't mean he wanted to come here tonight?" he demanded in outrage.

She laughed excitedly.

"Oh, I made it clear to him that was out of the question."

CHAPTER 10

Ben Safford got back to his office after an early afternoon quorum call in time to catch Madge and Janet red-handed.

"Mm-m-m." Perched on the corner of his desk, Madge was nodding vigorously as he entered. "And a haircut, too . . . Oh, here's the congressman now, Mrs. Lundgren."

Ben accepted the receiver with a grin and ran his left hand over his hair. It felt fine to him. Ostentatiously ignoring the gesture, Madge collected some papers and left.

"Hi, Janet," said Ben. "Why do I need a haircut?"

He should have known better.

"And probably a new tie, too," she replied bracingly. "I wish you had time to get a new suit . . . but, I've gone into all that with Madge."

Ben could tell when he was beaten. "Fine, fine," he said hurriedly. "How are things?"

Janet responded with a useful summary of Newburg opinion on the forthcoming Highway Fund vote, described local feeling on several other topics, then came up with a question of her own.

"How's Charlie Knapp?" she asked.

"We-ell"—Ben swung his chair far back—"it's a long and complicated story . . ."

Without comment Janet listened to his account of Alison's behavior at Burlington & Avery. She was less reserved, however, about the NPA's recent activities in Chevy Chase.

"Good heavens!" she exclaimed, blending sympathy and indignation. "And on top of that, Charlie's simply got to come back to Newburg."

"Why?" Ben asked.

This time Janet was all indignation. "Well, Ben!" she said impatiently. "How long do you think his business can run itself? Fred was talking to Al Munger just today . . ."

Shirley Knapp had left her husband so many burdens, it was sometimes hard to remember he had a life and responsibilities far from Washington. Ben was reminding himself of this when he tuned in on Janet again.

". . . that man Carrington," she was saying acidly. "Just do your best not to get photographed with him!"

It took a minute for the penny to drop. Then Ben saw he was back where he had come in, on his way to the barber shop.

"What a shame to spoil a White House wedding this way!" Janet continued. "Especially when you think how much tomorrow means to everybody."

Ben did not know if she was commenting as astute political observer, or experienced mother-of-the-bride. With this wedding, it did not matter much.

"Around here," he said, "people are breaking their backs trying not to think how much tomorrow means to everybody."

That was putting it mildly.

Decades ago, a youthful Nathan Landry had arrived to represent a rural Tennessee district in the House. Now, he was Vice-President of the United States. In the years between, he had been ready with a helping hand, or fatherly advice, whenever and wherever needed. Countless senators and representatives, including Ben Safford, had received favors from Nat Landry. So, when the child of his old age became engaged, there was a bipartisan outpouring of affection. Landry's long career in public service was drawing to its close, and Ben was not the only one who wanted to see it end in a blaze of sunshine.

The President himself had started the ball rolling by insisting that the only place for Betty Jo's wedding was the White House itself. From February on, Betty Jo was plunged into a fairy-tale round of trousseaux and bridesmaids, of wedding gifts and thank-you notes. And, amidst the glitter and excitement, her father beamed.

Then, in June, the blow fell. Bribery exploded into murder, and Washington belatedly absorbed the fact that Nat Landry's girl was marrying a Carrington.

"By then," Ben told Janet, "it was too late to do anything. So the show's going on."

"I'm sure he's a nice young man," said Janet stoutly before moving to a more practical plane. "Anyway, don't forget to get your shoes shined. You might say that it's the least you can do."

Ben concurred.

"The bride's side," he told the usher the following afternoon.

"We're the lucky ones," said Val Oakes beside him. "Look at those poor fish over there."

Ben saw what he meant. In the original eager scramble for invitations, many Southerners had decided to exploit their Texas connections. As a result there was Lou Flecker, who usually blossomed at weddings, trying to appear as if he had never heard of Houston.

Val was going to look on the bright side if it killed him. "Thank God it's *this* son that Betty Jo's marrying."

"Why?" Ben asked, recoiling from a matronly elbow. "Does Carrington have another one in jail?"

"Who cares about jail these days?" Val asked rhetorically. "No, the older boy is named John Bowie Carrington the Fourth—and he's the spittin' image of his father." With a hiss, he added: "Watch it, Ben. Here comes a photographer!"

A Rolleiflex zoomed in on them. After the danger had passed, Val apologized for his benign smile. "You can't look as if you expect the happy young couple to go straight from here to Reno," he muttered. "So long as we're stuck, we've got to put a good face on things."

Certainly, this seemed to be the prevailing philosophy. The scene was as colorful and animated as if Shirley Knapp had never existed. In recent days, Nat Landry's well-wishers had been pointedly and exclusively hoping that the weather would co-operate to make everything perfect. These hopes, at least, were realized. It was a balmy beautiful day which found the Rose Garden at its best, a riot of color and scent. The ladies, however, were not eclipsed. There were small hats, each a bouquet in itself. Some younger women had harked back to the past with airy dresses and large shady hats complete with velvet streamers. Silk and organdy fluttered, voices buzzed and even the real flowers swayed lazily in the light breeze.

This idyllic prelude ended suddenly when four joyful chords heralded the beginning of the ceremony. All heads turned as the maid of honor and the bridesmaids passed by with youthful dignity. Then, at last, Betty Jo appeared on the arm of her father, floating in a cloud of white. Like every bride, she was beautiful. But the hum of pleasure was for her escort. Vice-President Landry was radiant with pride and happiness. Five hundred distinguished guests felt a great gust of relief. Now they could relax.

The vows were exchanged, the rings were exchanged and, when Betty Jo returned, she was with a tall, handsome husband.

"Twenty minutes from start to finish," Val noted with approval.

"What makes you think this is the finish?" Ben retorted.

Unwillingly, he hoisted himself to his feet to join the conga line snaking across the South Lawn into the White House. There the President and the First Lady were tendering their own tribute to the Vice-President. Surrendering pride of place to the wedding party, the President passed down the reception line and kissed the bride twice for the benefit of the photographers, then let himself be engulfed by the press with whom he exchanged mild quips. The First Lady dimmed her incandescent smile and pretended, almost successfully, that she was just another old family friend. And if there were moist eyes when the bride waltzed with her father, the presidential two-step with the prettiest bridesmaid almost had them cheering.

"A lovely wedding," said the voice of authority. "And Betty Jo looks very nice."

Val and Ben turned to greet Mrs. Hollenbach, accompanied by Congressman Milton Seeburg who was half a head shorter than she was.

"You look nice yourself, Elsie," said Val. He had an eye for things like pale green silk.

Ben agreed, although his admiration was roused by Elsie's other talents. He and Val had both let their surroundings cow them into accepting champagne from a circulating tray. There had been no such truckling by Mrs. Hollenbach, who held her customary martini, no doubt extracted by simple will power.

"And all things considered, John Carrington is behaving well," Elsie went on.

Involuntarily, Ben craned around. "Carrington? I don't see him."

"That," Elsie explained precisely, "is what I mean."

Now that he came to think of it, Ben realized that Carrington's sole appearance had been his obligatory stint in the receiving line. "He's smart to lie low. Janet reminded me that he's embarrassing too many people today. Of course, the father of the groom can do a lot of ducking. We'd all be in the soup if he were the father of the bride."

Elsie looked pityingly at him. "If Carrington were the father of the bride, this wedding would be taking place two thousand miles away, and we'd all be better off."

Milt Seeburg was also willing to give the devil his due. "The guy's poison right now," he said, removing a large cigar from the corner of his mouth. "Still, you've got to hand it to him. He's trying—"

"I heard that!" The voice came out of the throng swirling around them before Warren Praeger marched straight into the panatela. "That's what Mildred was saying, too," he said, brushing his sleeve furiously. "I told her that I'd like to see John Carrington cooperating about something more important than his son's wedding—"

"And where," Elsie broke in with gracious implacability, "is Mrs. Praeger?"

Neither this, nor Milt Seeburg's baleful gaze, penetrated.

"Oh, she's dancing with someone," Praeger said with a vague bob toward the ballroom. "As I was saying, I'd like to see Carrington—"

Val Oakes succeeded where Elsie and Seeburg failed. "Doesn't sound like a good idea to me," he said lazily. "The way things stand, Warren, the farther you keep away from him, the better."

Praeger reddened painfully, but he could not let the subject alone.

"That is exactly the point I want to make," he said fussily. "In fact, I am going to make an official complaint about it. Someone from the NPA tried getting in to see me yesterday." Finally, he was getting the response he wanted. Swelling slightly, he continued: "Ben, can't you committee people put a stop to that sort of thing? I don't know what the NPA is trying to do to me!"

Warren Praeger's complaints had made Milt Seeburg study his ruined cigar with cold-eyed calculation. Both men were offending Val Oakes's sense of propriety.

"Let's drink to the young people's future," he suggested, flagging down a white-jacketed waiter.

But Warren Praeger's mouth reopened the minute the waiter moved on.

"That's fine, Val," said Ben quickly, "but you have to admit that the NPA sure seems to be covering a lot of ground these days." After a token sip, he briefly described the NPA's descent on Chevy Chase. "Charlie Knapp was steamed up about it," he said thoughtfully. "I told him I'd do what I could, but hell! I'm no expert in keeping people out. Thank God, Madge does that for me."

"You may have to start learning," Elsie warned. When Ben looked at her in mystification, she added: "Even Madge needs help now and then. For example, she needed it this morning. A Mrs. Underwood from the NPA came to your office."

It was enough to make any politician stiffen. Even Val swiftly abandoned sentiment for cold reality. "What did she want?" he asked.

"That's what Madge and I wondered," Elsie replied. "Madge asked me to sit in, Ben, but it soon became clear that this Underwood woman was trying to get information. She was particularly interested in how many documents Alison Knapp has given the committee"—Elsie's dramatic pause was deliberate—"so far."

While Warren Praeger made an indeterminate noise in his throat, Ben said: "Do you mean that the NPA is saying there's more than one memo from Shirley Knapp?"

Elsie was meticulous. "Perhaps I am conveying the wrong impression," she said. "This Mrs. Underwood volunteered no statements. She simply asked questions. However . . ."

Elsie's *however* was enough to make her colleagues think hard. In the ensuing silence, Ben was struck by a trivial thought: "How come this is the first I've heard about this?" he demanded.

"Possibly, because you were not at the House this morning," said Elsie. "Madge couldn't find any other member of the committee." She read the roster. "Tony had left for Providence, Lou Flecker was having an early lunch. Val was in the swimming pool, and Madge didn't know where you were. Or"—she smiled brightly at a passing bridesmaid—"she was unwilling to say."

Ben eyed her. Elsie was justly proud of her attention to duty. But, even so, she spent as much time away from the Hill as anybody else. She hounded agencies on behalf of her district, she entertained visiting firemen, she caucused, gave speeches, and chaired discussions. Still, she was always in the right place at the right time. Considering this, Ben had been forced back to the language of sports writers. Good players tried to be in the right spot. With your superstar, the ball simply came.

He was not going to plead extenuating circumstances. Ben had a fair idea of what he must look like by now. Why risk explaining that he had spent the morning making himself worthy of the White House, only to have Elsie reply that her high polish had taken ten spare minutes?

Val never tried measuring up to anyone. "Doesn't make any difference we weren't around," he concluded. "You probably handled this woman better than we could anyway, Elsie."

Milt Seeburg was not interested in compliments. "You said someone from the NPA approached you," he said abruptly to Praeger. "Was it Mrs. Underwood?"

Praeger blinked at this unexpected attack. "I have no idea," he said nervously. "It was someone from the NPA—that's all I know. What difference does it make? I have nothing to say to anyone from that organization."

"Just asking."

Seeburg was perfunctory enough to offend Praeger who decided that it was time for him to find Mildred. After he had stalked off, Seeburg's eyelids drooped thoughtfully: "Warren's not handling this thing right," he said at last.

Ben had not bought a new tie to listen to electioneering.

"Praeger's trying to run away from trouble," he said, forestalling the pitch he could see coming. "Your boy Adelman likes to go out to meet it. It's just a difference in style."

Seeburg was unruffled. "That's not what I meant," he said softly, before he too detached himself.

"You know where he's going, don't you?" Val asked with vast resignation. "To find out if Herb Adelman's heard from the NPA."

"Well, Praeger's going to fill Macnamara in," Ben predicted. It was human enough. It was also depressing. "This new NPA end play is going to have us all rushing around . . ."

"Not now," said Elsie Hollenbach firmly. Fastening a gimlet eye on her colleagues, she said: "Obviously, we're going to have to find out what the NPA is doing. And we are going to have to find it out quite rapidly. But at the moment we are waiting, at least until the bride and groom have left."

Her commandment was buttressed by several hundred years of tradition. Not until the seven-tiered wedding cake had disappeared, not until the bridal bouquet had been caught by a distant cousin, not until the newlyweds reappeared in traveling clothes, was any concerted movement made.

Then, while a shower of rice filled the air, many young voices cried:

"They're off!"

"Thank God!" said many of their elders.

Mr. and Mrs. Reed Carrington were not the only ones making a fast getaway.

CHAPTER 11

John Carrington had earned a certain amount of gratitude at his son's wedding by impersonating the invisible man. Unfortunately he had also effectively insulated himself from the rumors circulating through the East Room. By the next morning he was probably the only person connected with Shirley Knapp's murder who still had not heard of the NPA's recent appearance at scattered locations.

But pulling the plug on his intelligence network was only partly to blame. Family responsibilities helped explain why he was still in the dark. Yesterday he had gone straight from the White House to the Madison Hotel and festivities for the Texas contingent. The sixty-odd people who had started the day by gathering at Houston airport, then trooping aboard a chartered DC-10 (which was not, as press releases stressed, an NPA plane), had made whoopee far into the night. Then at four o'clock in the morning he emerged from the bathroom to find his wife weeping over the dressing table.

"But, Lillian, you didn't act this way when the others got married," he said involuntarily.

"You don't understand!" she wailed. "Reed was my baby."

John Carrington put in an exhausting hour before they finally got to bed and looked it at the breakfast table. Lillian, on the other hand, was fresh as a daisy, deploring her departure via the DC-10.

"As long as we're here, why not show folks a good time? Not

just rush them up and back. We should all stay a couple of days."

She repeated this refrain through toast, coffee and the trip to the airport. One of Carrington's crosses was his wife's refusal to understand why, these days, it behooved the family to maintain a low profile.

"You're staying," she said discontentedly. "And you've already been here too long. How can I plan anything when I don't know if you'll be home? What about our barbecue? You've invited over two hundred people."

"Don't worry, I'll be home for the July Fourth weekend." Carrington did not bother to explain why he could be so sure. No congressman was subpoenaing anybody that day.

Fortunately their arrival produced a diversion.

"Look, there's Fred—and Cindy!" Lillian exclaimed as the limousine pulled up to the curb. She flung open the door. "Here we are! Isn't it just terrible the way we have to go back so early . . ."

In the lounge Carrington manufactured gallantries for other ladies with a king-size capacity to keep the party going. But they, at least, did finally embark. It was a man who decided to stay behind.

Judge Preston Briggs, who would never rise higher than the Federal bench, was a legendary figure. He had spent a lifetime in Houston, then a lifetime in Washington and was now well beyond the normal human span. He knew all the sons, all the fathers and had known their fathers before them.

In the course of a successful career John Bowie Carrington had made contacts and used influence, but he was the first to admit that his skills were nothing compared to those of the undersized man now proposing to accompany him back to Washington. In some ways Judge Briggs's presence was reassuring. Many important people who had turned up at the wedding to dance with Lillian had been too busy to have lunch with her husband recently.

"I've been doing some calling around, John," said the judge placidly. "To put it in one word, you're in big trouble."

"I don't need anybody to tell me that."

"First off, there's this Safford Committee. It's going ahead and there's no way on God's earth you can stop it. Not by pulling strings or anything else."

As Judge Briggs would have been the first string, Carrington could reply in all sincerity: "I haven't tried."

"That's good. But what you've been doing instead may be worse. Now's no time for foolishness. The boys on the Hill are getting ready to fight for their lives."

His wizened inscrutable face left Carrington wondering if those boys were Congressmen Macnamara, Praeger, and Adelman, or others. But no questions were asked. Like the Washington *Post*, Judge Briggs protected his sources.

"I know they're worried," Carrington was testy. "But what can I do about it?"

"No need to get rattled," the judge reproved him. "Anyway I don't want to talk about them, so long as you know how bad things are. I want to find out where you dug up this woman."

Carrington was genuinely taken aback. "Shirley Knapp? She'd been with us for five years. What difference does it make where she—"

"Not her," Briggs interrupted. "I mean this new one."

Carrington stared. "Who the hell are you talking about?"

This time the judge was not stern. Instead, he was warmly reassuring. "Now, John, I knew your family before you were born. I'm not turning my back on you now, just because things are getting a little rough. You'd better come clean."

Even a stupid man would have been worried by now.

"Preston," Carrington said harshly, "I've never been more serious in my life. I don't know what you mean, I don't know what you're talking about, and believe me, I want to know! Will you just tell me in plain English?"

The judge was not going to be stampeded. Reflectively he examined the man he had known for fifty years.

"All right," he said at last. "The word's gone out that you're trying to bury the Knapp mess by hiring somebody else to pull another fast one. I don't know who this woman is, but it doesn't take much to explain what she's up to—blackmail."

"Go on," Carrington ordered. "Tell me about this woman."

Dispassionately the judge continued. "She started by cleaning out Shirley Knapp's house. I suppose that's where she got her ammunition. The timing's a little confused after that. Nobody wants to ask too many questions. But she did a runaround of congressmen, including Warren Praeger. Then she ended up at Safford's office, making damned sure he wasn't there. That was to give herself a little muscle, I guess. Stands to reason that he's the last one she really wants to see."

"Barbara Underwood!" Carrington said to himself incredulously. Bewildered, he turned to the judge. "Sure, she works for the NPA. But for God's sake, she's just the girl who was Shirley Knapp's secretary!"

"And you still say you don't know what she's up to?" Briggs asked shrewdly.

Carrington might have been fighting his way through a swamp. "I knew she'd been out to Shirley's house," he said slowly. "Safford's office was raising Cain about that. Between you and me, I was glad to see the stuff she collected. Not that there was anything important."

Judge Preston Briggs looked at him compassionately. "Son, if you really don't know all this little lady's been doing, you'd better find out—and fast!"

"What do you mean, Mrs. Underwood isn't in the office?" Carrington stormed.

The receptionist cowered. This was not the suave Carrington she had come to know. "Mrs. Underwood hasn't been in much lately," she quavered. "She says she has to go to appointments outside, now that Mrs. Knapp isn't here to handle them."

"Since when has she been doing Mrs. Knapp's job?"

This was so unfair that the receptionist plucked up her courage. "I just answer the phone here, Mr. Carrington," she snapped back at him.

It was a notable first. In the midst of his anxiety and anger, Carrington recognized that his control was slipping. Falling back on habit, he summoned a shamefaced smile.

"Sorry I barked at you. It's not your fault." Then the sugar went out of his voice. "But be sure and send Mrs. Underwood in to me the minute she shows up, will you?"

He had scored on two counts. His apology had more than undone the damage. And his promise of retribution for Mrs. Underwood was a glorious tidbit for the coffee break.

"Just wait until he gets a hold of her," the receptionist prophesied gleefully. "He's boiling."

"I told you she hadn't been promoted. She's simply been taking a lot of time off." The file clerk had spent the last week enviously watching Barbara zip in and out of the office.

"Oh, Mr. Carrington wouldn't bother with a little thing like that," said the receptionist.

"Do you suppose she'll be fired?" someone asked.

But John Carrington was thinking along more drastic lines as he paced back and forth. "I'll shake the truth out of her," he growled. "One way or the other, I'm going to find out what she's got up her sleeve."

His assistant tried bringing the temperature down.

"It may not amount to much," he cautioned. "After all, we saw what she found in Chevy Chase and that didn't have any surprises."

"We saw what she showed us," Carrington corrected him. "She could have held onto anything, including a signed memo from Shirley to the guy she bought."

By now the assistant was not betting on what either Mrs. Knapp or Mrs. Underwood might have done. He was still not sure where John Carrington stood.

"It could make things very awkward for the NPA," he began, "if Barbara Underwood knows who took that fifty thousand, and we don't."

"Don't kid yourself," Carrington said bluntly. "It's dynamite if she knows, regardless of what we know."

The assistant suppressed a sigh. No matter what other mistakes John Carrington might make, he still knew how to field questions inside his own office. And he could do it while he was thinking about something else, as he proceeded to demonstrate.

"Whichever way you look at it, Mrs. Barbara Underwood is stirring up plenty of mud for us. Everybody in Washington assumes she's acting with the blessing of the NPA."

Sometimes the assistant was too glib. "That shouldn't be hard to handle," he said calmly. "If she's trying to line her pocket, it's pretty clear she's acting on her own."

"You mean we just remind people we're in the business of paying out, not taking in?" Carrington sneered.

The assistant saw his mistake too late. "We could fire her," he faltered.

"And claim she was acting beyond her authority?" Carrington swung impatiently away as if disgusted. "We've gotten all the mileage out of that one that we're going to get. What bothers me is how long our members will let this ride. So far they've stayed clear, hoping everybody will forget about them. But sooner or later, they're going to start yelling."

He did not have long to wait. The NPA had a total membership of nearly a thousand privately owned power companies. Before five o'clock, twenty-three of them called to make their pitch. They were uniformly disturbed by bulletins from Washington, they didn't like the way things were going, they thought it was time to do something positive.

"It's got to stop, John," they said. "Hell, we kick in seventy-five thousand a year . . ."

"Sure, you've done a lot for us," they conceded. "But how much are you going to be able to deliver in the future . . . ?"

"What's the point in spending a fortune on TV spots about serving the American public if we get stabbed in the back by our own organization?"

The message came through loud and clear—from jovial gladhanders in Florida to chilly Brahmins in Boston. One way to refurbish the NPA's tarnished image was to start at the top. A new president and a new lobbyist . . .

"I think I'm going to call it a day," said Carrington wearily. "I'll be in early tomorrow."

But back in the lavish apartment rented by the NPA, he had barely poured his first drink when the telephone shattered his plans for an evening of relaxation.

"Mrs. Underwood?" he repeated in amazement. "You're damned right I want to talk to you!"

Barbara Underwood was just as anxious for a meeting as he was. "Good," she said brightly. "I've got lots to talk to you about. You'll be surprised at how busy I've been."

"That's what you think," he snarled.

Mrs. Underwood did not let his hostility faze her. "I know you've had a heavy schedule, too," she said understandingly.

"I'm sorry I didn't get to you earlier, but I knew you'd be busy with the wedding."

"Never mind about that."

"Still I think we should get together as soon as we can."

John Carrington slammed his glass down. "Like right now," he said grimly. "You can hightail it down to the office and—"

"That won't be necessary," Barbara interrupted crisply. "I'm just around the corner. I'll come up there."

When Carrington hesitated, she swept on. "I'll see you in ten minutes," she said, and hung up without waiting for a reply.

Her forecast proved slightly inaccurate. It was a full fifteen minutes before Carrington heard shrill screaming from the corridor. With one long stride, he reached the door and wrenched it open. For a moment, he looked directly into the horrified face of his next-door neighbor. Then his eyes dropped.

Barbara Underwood lay crumpled at their feet with her arms outflung. A circle of blood was steadily widening around her head.

CHAPTER 12

Captain Rudolph Heyer looked at the man he was questioning. This was a far cry from their first encounter. Barbara Underwood was not with them tonight: instead, blaring sirens were clearing her path to the operating theater at Georgetown Hospital. Nor were they surrounded by the echoing silence of empty NPA offices. Lawyers and detectives kept up the level of background noise. But the biggest change of all was in John Bowie Carrington, himself. The practiced charm, the easy smile, the smooth evasions were all gone.

"I'll answer what I feel like answering," he rasped.

By and large, Heyer preferred the new Carrington. Trying to talk turkey to this one was less of a strain.

"I'm in the Homicide Squad," he said bluntly. "It's none of my business what the NPA is doing. So long as it doesn't involve murder, you don't have anything to worry about."

The reference to the National Power Association brought protests from the lawyers. Heyer paid no attention. Although Carrington had insisted his legal counsel be present, he was not letting them call the shots.

"Crap!" he exploded. "If someone's trying to frame me, I've got plenty to worry about."

"You think this was a deliberate attempt to frame you?"

"All I know is that someone tried to murder that Underwood woman right outside my door." Carrington ended his statement by viciously grinding out a cigarette stub.

Heyer noted the gesture. He decided that his witness might be lying about many things, but not about his anxiety. Carrington even looked different. His deep tan had taken on a yellowish cast and a dark shadow outlined his jaw. He had been chain-smoking since the police arrived.

Heyer had chosen an unhurried tempo. He expected to be here for a long time. "Is that how it looked to you—that the attack on Mrs. Underwood was a murder attempt?"

"Hell, at first I thought she was dead."

"John!" One of the lawyers broke in. "There's no need to tell the captain what you thought. Just give him the facts."

"Fine," said Heyer. "Let's go back to the beginning and start over."

Carrington, slumped in his chair, shrugged indifferently. "Sure. We can do it a hundred times. It's still going to come out the same."

"Did you see Mrs. Underwood today, before she showed up here?"

"No, I haven't seen her for a couple of days."

"And had you made an appointment with her?"

"No, I didn't. I didn't know what she was talking about when she called."

This had troubled Heyer the first time around. "I still don't understand," he said. "This is your apartment, isn't it? You've got an office downtown. Why didn't you meet her there?"

"First of all, this isn't my apartment—it's an NPA apartment. We keep it for visitors, and sometimes we throw a party here. Sure, I use it when I'm in town. But so do at least six other people."

"So this is just like the NPA offices?"

"No, it isn't." Carrington straightened and frowned. "Let me put it this way. Shirley Knapp's been here plenty of times. Our PR man drops by for a drink if we have something to discuss. But all that's on invitation. The clerical staff always stays downtown."

"Then why did you have Mrs. Underwood here?"

Carrington groaned. "I've explained that. It was five-thirty and I'd just come in. The phone rang and it was her saying she wanted to see me. She was a couple of blocks away . . ."

"So you asked her up?"

"No." Carrington sounded resentful. "Actually I didn't get a chance to say anything. She told me she was in the neighborhood and she'd be right over. Short of ordering her to stay away, I didn't have much choice." There was a pause. "You know the rest. I poured myself a drink and sat around waiting. The next thing I knew some woman was screaming her head off in the hall outside. I opened the door and—"

"Exactly what did you see?"

"This woman from next door was backed up against the wall, screeching like a fire engine. Mrs. Underwood was on the floor, covered with blood."

"There was nobody else in sight?"

Carrington dismissed the suggestion. "Absolutely nobody."

"Now think back. The fire stairs are just around the corner. Did you hear anything there, or in the elevator?"

"No." Carrington spread his hands helplessly. "I told you that woman was having hysterics. There could have been a herd of elephants on the stairs. Anyway, as soon as I saw all that blood, I came back inside and phoned the police."

"You kept your head," Heyer admitted. "If Mrs. Underwood lives, it'll be because you got an ambulance right away."

"Remember that when you're making a list of suspects." Carrington managed to grin. "And, before you ask, the next thing I did was call Livermore. I told him to get over here and bring the best criminal lawyer in town with him."

"So I noticed," Heyer observed. "You figured you were in for a hard time?"

"I'm not crazy. Shirley Knapp has her brains blown out at the airport. Now, her secretary is half killed on my doorstep. I didn't think the police were going to write this one off as a casual mugging."

"No, we weren't," Heyer agreed. "Which brings us to the next question. What did Mrs. Underwood want to see you about?"

"Don't ask me. I haven't spoken with her all week. They told me she wasn't in the office much. But neither was I. The last couple of days, I've been busy other places."

"I know," said Captain Heyer levelly. "I saw the pictures of all your important friends at the White House. You don't have to remind me."

Carrington's blue eyes became chips of ice. "I'm not kidding myself, Captain. My important friends won't touch me with a ten-foot pole. God, they thought the wedding was embarrassing." He gave a short bark of laughter. "Wait until they hear about this."

The NPA's lawyer took this as an admission of weakness.

"Nonsense, John," he said sturdily. "Everyone realizes that Shirley Knapp got herself involved with some madman. That has nothing to do with you. You're simply an innocent bystander, and your friends will all see it that way."

"We can all make up reasons for the Knapp murder," said Heyer blandly. "But why Mrs. Underwood? What made her a menace to someone?"

"How should I know?" Carrington snapped. "I wasn't her boss. She took a few letters for me, made a few phone calls. But that's all."

"No, it's not," Heyer reminded him. "When Shirley Knapp disappeared, you ordered Mrs. Underwood to clean out the files, didn't you?"

"Don't answer that!" Both lawyers spoke as one.

Carrington cast them a look of cold dislike and continued to make his own decisions. "Sure I did. The Washington *Post* made it sound as if they had a pipeline to Shirley's files. I didn't know anything about her daughter then. It was only sensible to empty those cabinets while we had the chance."

The pressure was increasing.

"And Mrs. Underwood put everything through the shredder?"

"That's what she said."

"But it's possible she might have held onto something?"

"It's possible," Carrington said grudgingly.

"It's even possible there were files someplace besides the office?"

"Yes."

Heyer leaned back, studying his man thoughtfully. This was the point at which they had bogged down before.

"You say Barbara Underwood decided where you were to

meet. Do you think she was especially anxious to get into this apartment?"

Carrington did not bother with any disclaimers. He merely lifted his shoulders.

"You were with Barbara Underwood on the night of Shirley Knapp's murder. How did she sound after I left?"

"Get this straight, Captain. I didn't know what was in that woman's mind and I'm not making any guesses now."

Behind Carrington, his lawyers nodded in approval.

"You know, I've got men searching this apartment."

Carrington was openly truculent. "Go ahead. If you find anything, it will be news to me."

As if on signal, a uniformed patrolman stuck his head in the door. "We're through, Captain."

Heyer raised his brows in silent interrogation.

"Not a thing," the patrolman said.

"All right," Heyer clambered heavily to his feet. "But this is just the beginning. Before we're done, we'll know exactly where Mrs. Underwood fits in."

The lawyers waited until the door closed behind Heyer before bursting into speech. Carrington dismissed details with one curt obscenity.

"Skip the window dressing," he said. "Heyer believes one of two things happened. That woman found something out and I silenced her. Or else somebody stopped her getting to me. He wants to know what cards she was holding before he makes his choice."

Outside in the hall Heyer was saying much the same to his lieutenant. "It could go either way. And, from the looks of that woman, she isn't going to be talking to us for a long time—if ever. Have we heard from the hospital?"

"Just caught it on the radio, Captain. The fractured skull is the big problem. And even if they pull her through, they're not sure how much she'll remember."

In the elevator, Heyer was less confident than he had been upstairs. "Fitting Mrs. Underwood in is going to be hard as hell. We're not going to find one person willing to talk. Carrington was bad enough, but at least he's not running for election in a couple of months. Those three congressmen are going to—" He broke off as the elevator doors opened to a scene of turmoil. "What's going on here? Has a war broken out?"

The lieutenant was apologetic. "The television crews," he explained. "As soon as the name Carrington went over the wires, they were here in full force. We couldn't keep them out."

Heyer looked at the cables and cameras with dislike. "Pack of hyenas," he muttered.

Twenty-four hours later, Captain Heyer's opinion of television coverage was changing.

The girl was the first to arrive at headquarters. She was small, blond, and cuddly. She was also very excited.

"I talked to Congressman Adelman. He said to come down and tell you all about it."

"This is about Mrs. Underwood?" Heyer asked cautiously, rereading the note from the desk sergeant. She looked about fifteen to him.

"Well, that isn't what she called herself then. It was Ginny something."

"Maybe you'd better give me some background."

"I work for Congressman Adelman." She twinkled at his reaction. "I'm twenty-one. I've had this job for over a year. I'm receptionist and switchboard operator."

"Go on."

"About three or four days ago, I went out to lunch. Do you know that cafeteria across from Julius Garfinkle? The one with the health food?"

Captain Heyer had an encyclopedic knowledge of Washington's eating places. He even recalled the nut cutlets as he nodded encouragingly.

"This woman came and sat down beside me. Out of the blue she said it was much easier to shop at Garfinkle's now than when she worked at the New House Office Building. Naturally I thought she was a reporter."

For the first time Captain Heyer noticed that the sparkling eyes under the green eyeshadow were very intelligent.

"Had a lot of that sort of thing?" he asked sympathetically.

"And how!" She nodded so vigorously that her hair bounced on her shoulders. "Ever since the Shirley Knapp story broke.

And then, after Mr. Adelman's big press conference, they were around us like flies. But I decided she couldn't be press."

"Why not?"

The girl chose her words. "Somehow, she didn't have the same tone the others did. Do you know what I mean?"

"I think so."

"But it didn't take her long to get on to Shirley Knapp. She said how thrilling it must be to work in the middle of all the excitement. She was pumping me for all she was worth."

"So what did you do?"

"Talked and talked and didn't say anything," she replied promptly. "Just a lot of gush about how wonderful Mr. Adelman is, and what a nuisance the reporters are."

"I expect you've got a real technique by now." Heyer was openly enjoying himself.

She grinned impudently at him. "Well, the technique's a little different if it's a man. Then, I usually get a lunch out of it. But with this woman I was really curious. If she wasn't a reporter, what was she? So I tried to do a little pumping myself. I asked her name and where she worked. She called herself Ginny and said she worked in a building across the street. Then I let her steer the conversation so I could tell what she was trying to find out."

Heyer was rarely moved to compliments, but now he said: "Congressman Adelman is a lucky man."

"He isn't going to be much longer," she confided. "Not unless he raises my salary. That's my rule. Move up or move out!"

Barbara Underwood, Captain Heyer decided, had been playing out of her league with this girl.

"What conclusion did you come to?"

"It's hard to say," she led him on. "Of course, basically, she wanted to know if Congressman Adelman was the one who sold his vote. But she didn't seem to want to know anything specific —not unless you count questions about files."

She leaned back, preening.

"Files?" Heyer sat bolt upright.

"She gave me a big song and dance about her own boss across the street. He kept one file locked and she couldn't get into it.

Did I know how it was? She was all ready for the two of us to let our hair down."

"And how did you handle that one?"

The girl's eyes were brimming with mischief. "I said it sounded just awful. But that's all I got out of her. If you ask me, she was pretty confused about what she wanted herself. So I didn't think any more about it. Then, over breakfast this morning, I was watching the news and there she was, big as life. The announcer said she was Shirley Knapp's secretary. Well, that put a whole new complexion on things. Before, she could have been any kook. I raced into the office and told Congressman Adelman. And like I said, he shot me down here to tell you." She leaned forward curiously. "Does it help at all?"

"We'll have to work on it," he said frankly. Then he looked across the desk at his visitor and smiled so broadly that John Carrington would have had difficulty recognizing him. "But thank you very much for coming in. It was a real pleasure."

Heyer's next visitor was cut from a different cloth.

"Curtis," he introduced himself, flourishing a press card. "From the Washington *Post*."

"What's gotten into that desk sergeant?" Heyer complained. "We'll have a release for you boys later on."

He jerked a meaty thumb at the door.

"No, no!" Curtis protested. "You've got it all wrong. I'm here as a witness."

"That's a new twist. What are you a witness to?" Heyer was still doubtful.

Curtis planted himself in a chair. "It's this way. I saw a photo of Barbara Underwood on TV. The one who was clobbered outside the NPA apartment. I had a drink with her the other day, but she wasn't calling herself Underwood."

Heyer blinked.

"I think she was calling herself Nancy something at the time," Curtis continued. "I can remember it if I try. I never forget a—"

"The name doesn't make any difference," Heyer interrupted. "Where did you bump into her?"

"That's the funny part. A bunch of us were over at the Bureau of Naval Personnel to get a handout and listen to one of their PR briefings. This one was about WAVES being assigned to sea duty.

When it was all over we crowded into the elevators, and headed across the street for a drink. This girl was next to me in the elevator and came into the bar with the rest of us. She wasn't bad-looking, and I made room for her."

"You assumed she was part of the press corps covering the BNP?"

"That's it. I asked her who she was with, and she said *Mademoiselle*. That's when she gave me her phony name. I told her I was from the *Post*, and somehow we started on the Shirley Knapp business."

"Somehow!" Heyer scoffed. "There's a little girl running a switchboard who could give you lessons in this sort of thing. Tell me, did she sound like a reporter to you? Weren't you suspicious?"

Curtis was wounded. "Of course she didn't sound like a reporter. But I wouldn't expect someone from a fashion magazine to sound like a stringer. For all I know, *Mademoiselle* always covers the WAVES."

"Calm down. When she got you on the subject of Shirley Knapp, did you manage to figure out what she was after?"

"She didn't make any bones about it. She came right out and asked. Did the *Post* have anything else from Shirley's files besides the famous memo?"

Heyer nodded. "It follows. What did you tell her?"

Curtis had recovered his self-confidence. "I told her that if the *Post* did, they weren't telling me."

"And then she remembered she had an appointment, I suppose."

"No. She was turning out to be such a dog, I discovered I had another appointment." Curtis began to get up. "Anyway, I thought you'd like to know."

"Thanks. By the way, when did you see this picture on TV?"

Curtis was pleased with himself. "Six hours ago."

"Where have you been since? Over at the Navy?"

"Sure. I was trying to find out how she got in there. But they wouldn't give me the time of day. In fact, they ended up by throwing me out. So I wasn't able to save you any work."

"Don't let it worry you. I think I can figure it out by myself."

Captain Heyer's third visitor confirmed this guess, but was otherwise unhelpful.

"Yes, Barbara brought me my glasses a couple of days ago. I'd left them at home. I don't know how that happened." Commander Underwood was trying to co-operate but his distraction left him almost incapable of concentration.

Captain Heyer inquired about the latest news from the hospital and learned there had been no change. His gentle questions merely puzzled Barbara's husband.

"You don't understand," Lyman Underwood said finally. "Barbara just took that job to pass the time. You know, we don't have children, so she needed to occupy herself. Oh, I don't say the money doesn't come in handy. But basically Barbara is only interested in her home and her family."

This was probably true until two weeks ago, Captain Heyer thought. But there had been a big change in Barbara Underwood since then.

CHAPTER 13

In spite of attempts to fiddle with the calendar and create artificial three-day weekends, the Fourth of July remains the great American holiday, and everybody knows there is only one authentic way to celebrate it. First, the parade peacocks down Main Street with drum majorettes, bands, Boy Scouts, and Army Reserve units. Next comes a carnival with peanut butter fudge made by the Soroptimists and beer at the American Legion booth. At four o'clock there is a baseball game. Finally, when the last light fades into velvet darkness, the fireworks take over. Throughout there are speeches, awards to outstanding young people and, sometimes, community singing.

Congressman Benton Safford's place each year was an uncomfortable perch on an open convertible, proceeding from Court House Square through downtown Newburg and out to the County Fair Grounds.

"Fine turnout," remarked Mayor Wilhelm, who was flourishing his straw boater at the crowd as vigorously as if he were not nearing eighty years old.

Ben, waving and grinning for dear life, agreed that the mob seemed to get bigger each year.

Maybe it was just population growth. If you could believe the National Safety Council, there were thousands hitching boat trailers to station wagons, merging perilously onto throughways and heading as far away from it all as possible. But there were always more than enough left to overflow the parking lot, the midway and the Ladies Guild tent. And while new wrinkles were added each year at the Fair, they never succeeded in displacing the old standbys. A Space Ride for the Kiddies rubbed shoulders with the merry-go-round. A rock band alternated numbers with a square dance caller. Tomato preserves made by the Four-H still sold briskly against all sorts of new competition. The Flea Market, with its bewildering array of china and brass and quilts, had been going strong for some time. The latest innovation seemed to be the Craft Exhibition. Newburg, it developed, boasted a surprising number of amateur potters, weavers, candle dippers, and jewelry makers.

"Not a bad show," said Fred Lundgren, when Ben ran into him in front of D'Amico's Pizza, Submarines and Cold Drinks.

"Hi there, Phil!" said Ben as D'Amico emerged with a slice of pepper-onion-mushroom and a root beer. "How's business?"

Carefully wiping big hands down the front of an apron that had been white many hamburgers ago, Phil D'Amico replied with a squeeze of Ben's shoulder. From behind the grill, where she was expertly scraping sizzling onions, Angie D'Amico told Congressman Safford exactly how things went with the D'Amicos, as well as their connections—the Russos, the Gattos, the Toros, and, thanks to Angie's younger sister, the McIlheneys.

It was a scene to gladden Janet's heart when she rounded Folson's French Fries. If ever there was a time for a politician to have his mouth full, it was here in full sight of the electorate, listening to the voluble Mrs. D'Amico who held thirty-five votes in her spatula. Janet had long maintained that Ben's cast-iron stomach could be regarded as one of his qualifications for public office.

But the telltale lift of her right eyebrow warned Ben that she had something on her mind. One glance told him what it was. Trailing in Janet's wake were the Spanners. Dr. Spanner was a dentist, pure and simple. Mrs. Spanner, however, was civic-minded.

"Mr. Safford is our congressman," she said with a bright, prompting smile to her four children. "Now, do we all know what Congress is?"

The three boys were mutinously silent, but the pig-tailed little girl piped up obediently: "Congress is where they make the laws."

There were forced smiles from the captive audience.

"Yes, dear," beamed the proud mother. "And that is why it is so important for us to elect good men, not bad, selfish men."

"What the hell was that supposed to mean?" asked Fred belligerently once the Spanners had been safely left behind.

"God knows! I'm just thankful that baby-kissing has gone out of style," said Ben, halting to exchange greetings with Arthur Wu, one of his favorite downtown merchants.

"How can you say that, Ben?" asked Arthur, producing a broad round-robin smile that embraced them all. "You patted that little girl's head like a pro. I was waiting for you to rumple the boys' hair."

Janet did not have a monopoly on Safford family realism.

"If I'd laid a hand on them," Ben said unresentfully, "they'd have kneed me in the groin."

"And who's to blame them? With that mother, they've got a lot of aggression to work off," Arthur retorted.

Janet was changing the group's course. "Let's take a coffee break," she suggested. "The tent is just ahead. You'll come too, won't you, Arthur?"

But Arthur was about to go on duty at the Chamber of Commerce booth. "I'm relieving Charlie Knapp now. Why don't I send him over instead?"

Ben waited until they were seated at the planked tables and he had dutifully chatted with Mrs. Villars, the volunteer waitress.

"I didn't know Charlie Knapp was back home," he began. "Is it just for the weekend?"

"Yes, he and Arthur almost always run the CC show. They see a lot of each other because Charlie is down at Wu's Village for dinner a couple of nights a week."

It stood to reason. Very few bachelors—honorary or otherwise—can afford to develop a dislike for fried rice. But that was not causing Janet's frown.

"It was seeing Charlie that set Libby Spanner off," she explained. "About corruption in Washington."

"I'll bet it did." Ben was happy he had not been there. "And what's her position on corruption in Washington?"

"Confused," said Janet tartly. "But she thinks it's a terrible state of affairs that, while innocent women are being murdered, the chief suspects are waltzing at the White House. And," she went on conscientiously, "that the Safford Committee doesn't seem to be doing anything but joining the waltz."

"I did not do any waltzing at the White House," Ben defended himself.

"I'm glad to hear it." Janet was recovering fast. "But there's no doubt the attack on that Mrs. Underwood has made people impatient to have this thing cleared up. And your committee doesn't seem to be helping much."

Janet was not criticizing. She knew all the reasons for a go-slow policy until the wedding was over. She was merely reporting feeling in the 50th District.

"Well, our hearings start the day after tomorrow," Ben replied. "But I wouldn't get your hopes up. Congressional committees aren't supposed to solve murders."

Fred was arguing that activity, however futile, would quiet all but the diehards when Charlie Knapp appeared, already carrying a coffee mug.

"Hi folks! Arthur told me you were here," he said, reaching for the sugar. "You giving us a speech later, Ben?"

"A short one," Ben promised.

"You're not the problem," Charlie said honestly. "It's Wilhelm. When he gets on a platform, nothing can shut him up."

This was the first time that Ben had seen Charlie when he was not operating as husband to Shirley or father to Alison. He was a different man as he answered Fred's questions about the business. He had gotten more done in the last two days than he had expected. The payroll was met, billings straightened out and estimates prepared for mailing. Knapp Construction could survive another absence.

"And Billy's getting his first look at Newburg," Charlie added, sounding pleased. "He doesn't think it's so bad. He went swimming with the Clark kids yesterday, and he's around here somewhere with them now."

Janet commented that it was a good thing the Clarks, with their five children, lived next door and promptly invited the Knapps to dinner. But they were already booked at the Wus.

"Oh well, we'll make it next time," she said. "It sounds as if Billy could settle right down in Newburg. He's at a good age for making new friends. So if Alison wants to stay on at TJU . . . ?" Her voice trailed off inquiringly.

The first shadow of the day crossed Charlie's face. "Who knows what that girl wants," he said crossly. "If you ask me, she doesn't know herself. At least not for five minutes running."

"That's often the way at that stage," Janet murmured.

Charlie responded to her air of experience. "For instance, two weeks ago she was hot on getting an apartment in Washington when Billy and me leave. Staying on with her crowd at TJU was the big thing. She'd signed up for summer courses and everything. Then, a week ago—that's all over! Overnight, she wants to go to Europe. What's more, she doesn't know when she'll be coming back."

Ben opened his mouth, then shut it again. Meanwhile Charlie continued to unburden himself.

"Hell, I know they all like to travel nowadays. I don't say I'm against it. But she's got to make some plans. And stick to them for more than a couple of days. If she wants to try a year at a European college, maybe we could swing it. But I'm not laying out a lot of cash when she won't take the trouble to figure out what she's going to do. And another thing," he said, making Ben's point for him. "I don't know how the police would like it if she just disappears into the blue. They're in the middle of investigating her mother's murder."

"You've got something there," Ben agreed. "I think Heyer would appreciate a little warning."

Charlie examined his congressman appraisingly. "And it's not just the police, is it? I seem to remember that you've served a subpoena on Alison, too, haven't you?"

"That's right. I don't think we'll call her unless the NPA contests the memo and that doesn't seem likely. But frankly, Charlie, it wouldn't be a good idea for Alison to make herself scarce right now. Not with so much riding on these hearings."

Warren Praeger had spent World War II as a lawyer in the Judge Advocate General's Corps. This had consisted of desk duty for three years in Chicago. But since 1945 the details of this military career had grown dim. Praeger's annual Fourth of July address to the Lincoln Chapter of the VFW had become more and more suggestive of active combat. This time was no exception.

"Those of us who defended the ideals of our country on the field of battle have a special duty to continue that mission in our lives as private citizens. The preservation of all we hold dear is our responsibility. Our fallen comrades demand no less of us."

He sat down to a gratifying burst of applause.

"Nice going, Warren," said the man next to him. "That should shut everybody up."

Praeger put down the glass from which he had taken a refreshing gulp. His companion, he saw, had not been confining himself to water. "What do you mean, Harvey?"

Harvey was too triumphant to be diplomatic. "Some of the boys thought maybe we should have another speaker this year. The way things stand."

Over a long career, Congressman Praeger had developed real talent at dodging the issue. "I know some of the younger men think we're pretty old hat," he said deliberately misunderstanding. "They don't understand that war marks a man for life. Fifteen, twenty years doesn't make any difference—"

"No, that wasn't it." Harvey was still drinking. "It was the Shirley Knapp murder. And these hearings that are going to start. They don't like the smell of it."

Warren Praeger knew there was only one thing to say and he said it. "Then, I disagree with them." He drew himself up. "Personally, I look forward to the hearings. I welcome the opportunity to testify."

In Brooklyn, for the first time in his short career, Herbert Adelman was addressing a major meeting of B'nai Brith. And he was doing so as the big drawing card of the evening. This new prominence was causing readjustments on many fronts. His mother received the shock of her life when she arrived to find her daughter-in-law graciously greeting old acquaintances and making new ones. Irene—putting people at ease! Four short years ago, Mrs. Adelman, senior, had been dismayed at her son's choice.

"I don't say she isn't a lovely girl. I don't say she wouldn't make a good home," she had protested. "But is she the wife for somebody who wants to go into politics? She's so shy she can't get two words out."

It was not easy to admit that, when it came to the crunch, Irene was being a real asset. For that matter, Mrs. Adelman had no intention of admitting it. She moved through the reception in a confused haze of relief and resentment. But when the speeches began, every feeling yielded to maternal pride.

Herb Adelman briefly touched the traditional Fourth of July topics before getting down to brass tacks.

"Yes, government *by* the people," he said. "The power is there, but it cannot be exercised without information. And what have we been witnessing in Washington during the past three weeks? A massive blockage of information. There should be an end to this cover-up. We must demand, as our right, an immediate and complete investigation into the activities of the NPA. I would go further. Now is the time for a complete overhaul of the lobbying system that has done so much to prejudice proper legislation. With the disclosures of the Safford Committee as our opening gun . . ."

Herbert Adelman was not the first young congressman to welcome a campaign he could spearhead.

Big speeches were not Dick Macnamara's line. His low-keyed style was designed to mesh with the habits of his neighbors. Whenever possible, he preferred that he be seen in Concord as part of the Macnamara family. To this end, the Macnamaras spent every school vacation back in Massachusetts with the summer as their longest stay. The day that school ended, Kate Macnamara started working on logistics. By the Fourth of July they were always settled, ready to entertain and be entertained.

Saturday had found Macnamara at the town dump attending festivities in honor of new pollution controls. Amidst mountains of Coca-Cola cans and old newspapers, he cut the ribbon and commended the ecological concern displayed by the young. During the afternoon of the Fourth he had been on a reviewing stand. But that evening gave him the kind of exposure he liked best. He gathered with a large group of environmentalists for a walk through a bird sanctuary, followed by a marshmallow roast during the fireworks. Here he moved from one small knot to another, listening and occasionally giving his opinion.

No one had missed the connection between his morning at the dump and Section C.

"It's ironic," somebody sympathized.

"Not really. I plan to be increasingly active in the field of better environment," Macnamara said reasonably.

Several people joined them.

"I'm glad you're all here," Macnamara continued. "I'd like to explain exactly why I voted for the act but did not wish to include private power companies in it."

He spoke easily and persuasively.

Finally he smiled at his audience. "It's good practice for me. I'm going to have to go through all this with the Safford Committee, you know."

But he had lost their attention. A magnificent set piece exploded in the sky.

"O-o-oh!" they cried. "Just look at that one."

In his own way, John Bowie Carrington was also running for re-election. The guest list in Washington had been prepared months before the scandal broke. Not so with the magnificent barbecue around the Carrington pool outside Houston. These people had been handpicked. Carrington was reminding them that, no matter what happened in Washington, he was going to be a very important person in Texas for a long time to come.

As a matter of policy, he admitted the worst at once.

"These are hard times, I can't deny it. You should see the way they're scurrying around on Capitol Hill."

Here, he seemed to be saying, we don't panic that easily. Here, where men are men, we understand the biggest storms blow over.

"I suppose they're worried about these hearings," someone ventured.

Carrington was a very big man, who understood small men. "You can't blame them. They're all worried about their next election. After all, if they lose their seats, what have they got to go back to?"

Then, as if reminding them of what a Carrington could come home to, he playfully punched the arm of a member of the Texas

Railroad Commission. "You must be busy these days, Jesse. I see the new oil-lease ruling is going through."

In Houston when you thought about oil leases, you thought about John Carrington.

Jesse's response was cordiality itself.

"I wouldn't worry too much about these Safford hearings," Carrington said confidently. "You know what congressional committees are like. They may stir up a big rumpus at the time, but in the long run, what effect do they have?"

CHAPTER 14

"Washington in July!" said Tony Martinelli pugnaciously. "The next guy who tells me how much worse things were before air conditioning gets a punch."

Whenever Congress has to sit through the dog days, tempers grow short. Minor differences of opinion occasionally do escalate.

"Just thank the good Lord for small blessings," said Lou Flecker fearlessly. "We're going to need all the cooling off we can get!"

They were matching Ben Safford stride for stride toward Committee Room B, where hearings into allegations of misconduct by certain members of Congress were about to resume.

The Ad Hoc Committee was raring to go. The Fourth of July break had acted like an all-round booster shot. Elsie Hollenbach was not the only one who had returned to her duties in Washington with a glint in her eye, and explicit instructions for the hastily assembled committee staff. Even Val Oakes had been on his toes at the briefing session.

"Now's the time to put the screws on the NPA and Carrington," he had said, tugging at his lower lip. "If we lean on them, we're bound to get something. Not much—but something. How is that Underwood woman, by the way?"

Mrs. Barbara Underwood was still on the danger list. But her activities had given the Ad Hoc Committee some leverage.

"They're not dummies over at the NPA," Tony had said. "After what's happened, they'll try co-operating a little."

His wicked smile was not enough for Elsie. "We'll get more than co-operation from the NPA before we're through," she had said resolutely. "However, I think that the committee is obligated to tackle the three congressmen first."

There had been no enthusiasm, but no objection either.

"Here goes!" said Tony, stiff-arming the door to Committee Room B.

It did not surprise Ben to find Mrs. Hollenbach and Val Oakes ready and waiting. As he looked up and down the raised table, then out ahead of him, he was reminded of their final, unanimous decision: no three-ring circuses.

His work was cut out for him. Today, avid spectators filled every seat allocated to the public. The press was also out in force, straining forward to snatch revealing insights. Three artists were already sketching furiously. Thank God, thought Ben, bringing down the gavel with a crash, the House still barred TV cameras.

"This committee is now in session," he announced before the noise subsided. Then, as if charging a jury, he added: "We are investigating allegations of misconduct—specifically bribe-taking —against certain members of Congress . . ."

At least nobody laughed raucously. He wished he could believe this was respectful silence but he knew better. With one woman dead and another near death, it was more of an expectant hush.

Alphabetical order decreed that the first witness should be Congressman Herbert Adelman. As he made for the witness table, Ben was determined to prevent a replay of the now-famous TV appearance. But Adelman handled the preliminaries with model restraint.

As a result, they got to the tricky ground with breakneck speed.

"Now, Congressman," said Lou, spelling Ben. "You told us that as soon as you realized Mrs. Knapp was offering you a bribe, you broke off all communication with her. Is that right?"

"Despite her persistence," said Adelman, turning to face the end of the committee table. "She wasn't a woman who took no for an answer. She kept after me for weeks."

There was a stir of recognition at this echo of an earlier, more impassioned, Herb Adelman. Lou Flecker heard it too.

"Just tell us how far she committed herself," he directed. "Did Mrs. Knapp mention a specific sum of money?"

"She never mentioned money at all." Adelman acknowledged the buzz from the gallery by arching heavy dark brows. "She was more subtle than that. She said casually that the NPA had a vacant suite of offices in Brooklyn that they'd be happy to put at my disposal. Then, the next time we met, she told me that some NPA professionals—a PR man and a statistician, I think—were at loose ends. I could use them if I wanted. When she started talking about researchers and computer time, I finally got the picture. The NPA was offering to subsidize a whole office and staff."

Elsie Hollenbach was doing arithmetic. "That would come to more than a hundred thousand dollars a year."

He did not dispute her estimate. "I should have realized the implication of the NPA's offers sooner. I blame myself for being slow. In excuse, I can only plead total inexperience with this degree of corruption!"

"And that's one hell of a good punch line," said Tony Martinelli from behind a shielding hand.

It was also a hard act to follow. Congressman Richard Macnamara acknowledged this with a rueful smile to Adelman as they passed in the aisle. But confronting the committee he was impassive.

Like his predecessor he did not want anybody to think he had anything to hide. Without hesitation, he followed Ben through the weeks before the vote on Section C, from NPA cocktail parties to private meetings with Shirley Knapp.

"Somehow or other, we got talking about money," he said candidly, stroking a sunburned nose. "Maybe I said I needed more, I don't remember. I do remember it was the reception at the Indian Embassy. Mrs. Knapp got me into a corner—and came out with it."

"Did she offer you cash?" Ben asked.

"Not in so many words," Macnamara said dryly. "She called it an interest-free loan, with no hurry about repayment!"

His down-to-earth manner dampened the audience response.

"In what amount?" Ben asked, just as neutrally.

Macnamara crossed his arms. "She never got a chance to say. Frankly, I was stunned, and I let it show. Then I got away just as fast as I could!"

Elsie checked her notes. "And did she approach you after that?" she asked.

"Not on your life!" Macnamara was shaking his head. "I didn't make any bones about how mad I was." Suddenly, his face lightened. "But I wasn't running any risks, either. After that night, I made sure I was never alone with Mrs. Knapp for a single minute."

The Ad Hoc Committee adjourned for the day at four o'clock.

"Two down and one to go," Val announced, as they straggled back to Ben's office. "And so far, no skeletons . . ."

Unfortunately, staff investigators had been burrowing far from Committee Room B. Their findings were contained in a bulky folder guarded by Madge Anderson.

Ben took a cursory look through, then passed it along. "Well, you were right about one thing, Tony," he said, foreseeing a bad day ahead. "The NPA is willing to co-operate a little . . ."

Elsie's response to the photostats, receipts, and carbons was even bleaker. "No one ever said this was going to be a pleasant assignment," she said.

What made everything worse was the fact that Congressman Warren Praeger was impervious to warning.

He came to the witness table the next day armored, and blinkered, by his own self-esteem.

"No, Mrs. Knapp never made any such overtures to me. Of course, she argued the NPA position on Section C very forcefully. I was not fully decided as to how to vote. Since this was so, I listened to her, as I listened to many other interests . . ."

From an inside pocket, he produced a piece of paper and began reading a list.

"The record will so show," said Ben. "Now, among the people you listened to on the subject, was Mrs. Knapp. Did you see her frequently?"

"Yes indeed," Praeger was assured. "Over a period of two or three months, I saw her several times a week. But, as I have just indicated, I was consulting with other—"

"And during these frequent meetings, she never offered you a bribe?" Ben's harshness, which sprang from mixed motives, offended Praeger.

"Of course not," he said with dignity. "Mrs. Knapp knew very well that raising such a subject would have put our meetings to an end!"

Ben was staring hard at the folder before him when he asked his next question: "I am not referring to an outright offer to buy your vote. Did Mrs. Knapp promise you any favors?"

Praeger was lofty. "So she could suck me in? No indeed. I'm too old a hand to be caught that way."

The Ad Hoc Committee had agreed that Ben should not have to do all the dirty work himself. But now, at the critical moment, they were reacting differently. Lou Flecker was gnawing his thumb, while Tony Martinelli shifted restlessly in his seat. Mrs. Hollenbach folded her hands, as if in prayer. Val Oakes opened his eyes.

"Congressman Praeger," Ben said formally. "This committee has obtained access to records of the NPA containing information about certain expenditures. Would you care to make a general comment?"

Praeger blinked rapidly. "About what?" he asked slowly. "I have accepted NPA hospitality, if that's what you mean. So has everybody else."

Did Warren Praeger really think that semantics were going to save him?

"According to our information, you and Mrs. Praeger were guests of the NPA in Acapulco for two weeks in April last year." Ben had opened the folder to consult the first document.

"It was a research trip," Praeger said hotly, flushing as a ripple of laughter emanated from the gallery. "I was familiarizing myself with some aspects of offshore oil development. Mexico has—"

"How did you go down to Mexico?" said Ben, who did not want to prolong this.

"Why, by plane."

"Who paid for the tickets?"

"Payment did not arise," Praeger told him. "Several executives from the NPA were also going down. A company plane was used."

Ben let this pass. "And where did you stay?"

"The NPA owns several cottages on the grounds of the Royal Inn," Praeger said. "One of them was assigned to Mrs. Praeger and myself."

He was satisfied with himself until Elsie Hollenbach started in. "Can you tell us how big these cottages are?"

Praeger glowered, but Elsie was relentless. The cottage was an eight-room house on the golf course, complete with swimming pool and patio. After this Elsie extracted an account of gala parties every night from one end of Acapulco to the other. She wound up with the two maids and houseboy who had waited on Mr. and Mrs. Warren Praeger during this fact-finding mission.

Ben had to rap sharply for order before opening a new line of attack.

"Who arranged for you and your wife to join this party?"

"Mrs. Knapp," said Praeger, raking the table with indignant eyes.

"And you still do not regard it as a favor?"

"Nonsense," Praeger blustered. "It was only a common courtesy. It could have been offered to any congressman."

Derisive hoots from the onlookers goaded Lou Flecker into asperity. "But how many congressmen would have accepted?"

He then looked as if he could have bitten his tongue, and Ben hastily tried to make headway.

"Now, your stay in July last year at the Homestead—"

"Another courtesy," Praeger interjected. "The Homestead was reserved for a week of panel discussions and the NPA took a wing. Many of their member companies sent representatives, and several congressmen were invited to tell the business community about legislative matters . . ."

"Yes, there were other congressmen present," Ben allowed. He had their names, too. But both Peale and Forster were notoriously in the pocket of the oil industry.

Val Oakes's inning had come. He roused himself to make Praeger describe the NPA plane that ferried him back and forth between Nebraska and Washington, on call. After that, Tony covered the opulent hunting lodge in Wyoming, where John Carrington had hosted several oil executives, some Hollywood names —and Warren Praeger.

But it was Chairman Safford's job to put the pieces together. He glanced down at the witness table. In one short hour, Praeger had shrunk. His hands, clenching the sides of the chair, were white-knuckled. His voice was almost inaudible.

"Congressman Praeger," said Ben, wishing he did not have to. "How long have you served in Congress?"

"Fourteen years." Praeger was still grasping at straws. "That is why my conscience is perfectly clear. I know how things are done. These items you've chosen to bring up—I repeat, they are simply normal courtesies and nothing more."

Ben forced himself on. "In fourteen years, Congressman Praeger, you must have learned that lobbyists and interest groups —like Mrs. Shirley Knapp and the NPA—don't do things for nothing, even if they wait before they present a bill. How long was it until Mrs. Knapp told you that the NPA wouldn't go on providing the good things of life if you didn't vote against Section C?"

"Never!" Praeger howled. "We understood each other. She was simply keeping on good terms with me, that's all!"

"Why did she want to keep on good terms with you?"

"So she would be welcome when she wanted to present me with the NPA position." Praeger was trembling with emotion.

"So, you were making her pay for that privilege?"

Praeger was still fighting back. "Call it paying if you want," he spat. "That's all she got for anything she or the NPA may have done."

"Did she ever ask for anything more?" Ben pressed.

"*No!*"

"Did she ever offer you anything more—like a lump sum?"

"No, no!"

In her way, Elsie was tougher than the rest of her colleagues put together.

Unpityingly she regarded her victim. "Congressman Praeger," she said, "did Mrs. Knapp ever suggest to you that the NPA was willing to make a sizable contribution to your campaign chest?"

There was a painful silence. Then Warren Praeger showed he had reached his sticking point.

"She did not!" he said, ashen with fury. "And I resent the implication! I accepted small courtesies from Shirley Knapp and nothing more!"

Under his hand, Ben had enough material to continue this ordeal almost indefinitely. But what the record would show and what the stomach could take were two different things. Ben thought briefly of World Series tickets, weekends in New York and a new heating system for the house in Lincoln, Nebraska.

Then, without consulting anybody but himself, he came to a decision.

"This meeting," he bellowed with a mighty heave of the gavel, "stands adjourned!"

CHAPTER 15

Before Ben's gavel sounded twice, every chair at the long committee table was being pushed back.

"Let's remember," Elsie said, with a jaundiced look, "that there are cameras waiting out in the hall. Ben, we should say that it's premature to comment on the testimony we have heard so far—"

"And do our best not to look sick," Val finished irrepressibly. "I wonder if Warren has enough sense to keep quiet himself."

Elsie opted for action by leading the way into the jaws of NBC, ABC, and CBS.

They smelled blood.

"Mr. Oakes! Would you give us your impression of these disclosures . . . ?"

"Have you finished questioning Praeger, Congressman Safford?"

"There he is! Mr. Praeger! Will you give us a few words . . . ?"

The Ad Hoc Committee shook off the sniping in good order and doggedly plowed away from Committee Room B.

"Jesus Christ!" exclaimed Tony. "No, don't look at me like that, Elsie. They're not after us. They're all back there, listening to Warren . . ."

Safely around the corner, Val Oakes stopped the procession and let loose.

"You know, I never thought Warren was real bright," he pontificated, "but now I'm beginning to think he's so dumb that it's dangerous! You mean to say he's telling the whole story all over again—for TV?"

Congressman Flecker took a cautious look back.

"Somebody is," he reported dolefully.

Val groaned aloud. But Tony had an explanation.

"Praeger probably thinks he can sell it with a big personality play. You know, a lot of sincerity—and then that pile of dead fish he's carrying will smell like a fancy bouquet," he said sarcastically before setting off toward his office.

"What I need now," said Val Oakes with simple sincerity, "is a drink. But what I'm going to get is a long speech by two dummies from HEW who think that they can tell me a lot about the Food Stamp Program in South Dakota."

Shaking his head ponderously, he lumbered off, followed reluctantly by Lou Flecker.

"I've got two Sons of the Daughters of the American Revolution waiting in my office," he said in sad valediction.

"Who says congressmen don't earn their pay?" Ben remarked to Mrs. Hollenbach. "Elsie, I still feel exposed out here. Come on into my office."

It was universely conceded that Elsie never needed a drink in the same therapeutic sense that her male colleagues did. Nevertheless, she immediately accepted Ben's invitation.

"After Warren Praeger's performance," she said with rare weakness, "yes, Ben, I will join you . . ."

"Oh, Mr. Safford! *And* Mrs. Hollenbach!"

Madge's welcome, beamed at them from the doorway, was just mechanical enough to convey a message. "Before you go into your office, Mr. Safford . . ."

With an inward *damn*, Ben deciphered. Hospitality was going to have to be delayed. Somewhere, someone was lying in wait.

Since Madge was as efficient as they come, this meant someone bigger than a passing constituent. But Ben was tired.

"Can't you handle it, Madge?" he said, cupping Elsie's elbow and forging on.

"I thought you might be interested, Mr. Safford." The baritone came from behind Madge.

Escort or not, Elsie halted when she chose. "Why, Captain Heyer," she said, reinvigorated. "What are you doing here?"

Heyer, with a paternal nod at Madge, explained that he was

getting the story on Barbara Underwood. "And this young lady was just telling me that you were here, Mrs. Hollenbach," he continued ingratiatingly.

It was, as Ben could have told him, a waste of cunning. Any opportunity to discharge her civic duty was an alarm bell to the firehorse in Elsie; today, after Warren Praeger, she was champing at the bit.

"Why don't we all go inside," said Ben, bowing to the inevitable.

"Fine," said Captain Heyer.

Ignoring the desk, Ben headed for the corner near the window with a sofa and chairs. These, thank God, were not proceedings over which he had to preside.

But the man calling the shots was playing it very easy.

"Since Mrs. Underwood got attacked," he began conversationally, "we've been looking into her activities . . ."

Dominating the conversation may be child's play for any experienced police officer—but not with Elsie Hollenbach present.

"Just a moment, Captain Heyer," she said with her usual authority. "May I ask a question?"

"Certainly," said Heyer, as if he had any option.

To do Elsie justice, she would have interrupted even if she had never won a primary.

"John Carrington," she said briefly. "I gather you do not have enough evidence to justify arrest?"

Heyer shrugged.

"Despite the fact," said Elsie penetratingly, "that Mrs. Underwood was attacked on his very doorstep?"

"That's right," said Heyer phlegmatically.

Elsie played her trump. "I see," she said, with a shade of menace.

This time Heyer waited in silence, thus earning good marks from Ben. Many a four-star general and Cabinet Secretary found it impossible to keep from dancing when Congresswoman Hollenbach piped the tune.

"What I'm looking into now," Heyer began again, "are some new leads. Particularly in connection with what Barbara Underwood was doing after Shirley Knapp got killed. We can't ask her

—and the doctors don't know when we can, or even if she'll be able to tell us much."

"Always assuming that she would be willing to," said Elsie indefatigably, surprising Heyer into a quick, respectful look.

"Yeah," he said. "Now, Miss Anderson was describing how Mrs. Underwood behaved when she came here. The reason we want to know . . ."

As always, Elsie had left her mark. Heyer now felt it necessary to prime the pump with a résumé of Mrs. Underwood's activities.

Some, like the girl from Herb Adelman's office, Ben had already heard about. Adelman himself had been fulminating about it to anybody who would listen. Others, like Curtis from the Washington *Post*, were new to him.

"So you can see why we're digging," Heyer concluded on a note of invitation.

Madge, under Elsie Hollenbach's surveillance, responded.

"She identified herself as Mrs. Underwood—from the NPA," she said, knitting her brows to help recapture the scene. "She asked how many exhibits the committee was planning to use . . ."

Heyer turned to Ben. "And you weren't here, Mr. Congressman?"

"No," said Ben. "The first time I heard about it was from Mrs. Hollenbach at the wedding."

Heyer squinted through smoke. "Kind of a funny subject to talk about at a White House wedding, wasn't it?"

Madge's hand went over her mouth in an involuntary gesture. Fortunately for everybody's peace of mind, Mrs. Hollenbach had either not heard—or did not believe that anybody could question her social behavior.

"The subject arose," she explained precisely, "because of Congressman Praeger. He was telling us that NPA people had been trying to see him . . ."

There was enough vitriol in her voice to let Madge know that the hearing had been a doozy. Captain Heyer, who presumably would read all about it in the evening paper, concentrated on substance not style.

"Just brought it up at the wedding like that, did he?"

"Yes," said Elsie repressively. When she co-operated, she co-operated to the hilt. "That, in turn, is when I described Mrs. Underwood's visit to this office."

Ben tried his own hand at bird-flushing.

"You can see why it was interesting. Not that we knew what was going to happen. But Mrs. Underwood had already been out to the Knapp house in Maryland to go through Mrs. Knapp's files . . ."

"Yes, I remember your telling us—" Mrs. Hollenbach agreed, breaking off to stare at Heyer.

He was having a paroxysm.

"Smoke gone down the wrong way?" Ben asked. Madge, the practical one, rose to get the carafe of water.

"What was that about Barbara Underwood going out to Maryland?" Heyer wheezed hoarsely.

Ben relayed the facts as known to him.

"Fine!" Heyer snorted. "The kid tells Charlie Knapp, Charlie Knapp tells you. You tell half of Washington—at the White House, no less. Why doesn't somebody tell the police? My God, we've had pictures of that woman on television. We've been asking for information—any information! And nobody sees fit to mention it."

The heat was going on Charlie, Ben could see, unless he'd had the good sense to stay in Newburg.

Elsie was still occupied with loose ends. "That," she said, "was the extent of our discussion of Barbara Underwood."

Heyer wheeled to Madge so abruptly that the water she was pouring spattered Ben's desk.

"And the next morning, I suppose you heard all about it."

"The next morning," said Madge, absently searching for mopping material, "everybody on the Hill had heard about it. Do you want a glass of water?"

"Or something stronger?" said Ben, rising himself.

"Good heavens!" said Mrs. Hollenbach, cocking an ear. "What's that?"

The closed door between Ben's sanctum and the outer office muffled sound but, even through that filter, voices raised in anger were unmistakable.

"Oh honestly!" Madge exclaimed irritably. "Will you excuse me . . . ?"

When it came to shouting, Ben was old-fashioned.

"Wait a minute, Madge," he ordered, getting to the door a step ahead of her. "Maureen may need—"

As he pulled, somebody pushed. Still protesting, Maureen fell into the office.

"But you can't . . . Mr. Safford's busy . . . oh-h-h—Madge!"

"It's all right, Maureen," said Ben, straightening wearily. "Just stop wailing, will you? Now, what the hell . . . ?"

Charlie Knapp was going from strength to strength.

"Glad to see you, Charlie," said Ben, standing back to let Madge lead Maureen away. "But did you have to shoot your way in?"

Charlie was poking a thick forefinger into Captain Heyer's chest.

"Just the guy I want to see!" he said truculently.

"Oh yeah? Well, that's a coincidence—"

Elsie Hollenbach took a hand. "If you will both sit down," she said quellingly, "we might be able to discuss things like adults. And Ben, I believe that we could all use that drink . . ."

By the time Madge slipped back in, calm prevailed, although Charlie showed signs of erupting again.

"What do you mean, I'm getting excited?" he growled. "She's nineteen years old . . ."

"That's what I said!"

Elsie, tossing off her brandy like a sea dog, continued to exert the absolute tyranny of the third grade teacher.

"Alison Knapp," she explained to Madge, "did not come home last night. Her father is naturally anxious and he wants police action. Captain Heyer has been pointing out that there is no need to be overly alarmed—"

Heyer was at the telephone, relaying orders to headquarters. No matter what anyone said, there was plenty of cause for concern.

"All right," said Heyer, returning to the sofa. "We'll probably find that she's spending the night with a girl friend—or a boy friend."

When Knapp refused this consolation, Heyer's voice hardened: "If you've been so damned worried, why didn't you call the cops yourself? What did you expect Congressman Safford to do?"

But Charlie was no Warren Praeger, caving in under hostile questions.

"I've been going crazy trying to figure out what to do," he said unashamedly. "I finally decided Ben might be able to help."

Ben thought he saw the problem. "We can't be sure this is a police case. Alison has had some trouble readjusting. She may have taken off on her own."

"Mm," said Heyer, digesting this. "Well, we'll check that out, too. In the meantime, what's this about Mrs. Underwood coming out to your place in Chevy Chase?"

He listened intently to Charlie's bald account, then got ready to leave.

Ben escorted him to the corridor.

"A lot of things can happen to young girls in Washington," he said tentatively.

"Especially young girls mixed up with this Shirley Knapp affair," Heyer replied forthrightly. "Has she been in touch with you recently?"

Shaking his head, Ben asked: "What if she's just walked out?"

"We'll find her," said Heyer. "We've been on this case for weeks now—and we know more about Alison Knapp than she thinks. She's an ordinary kid."

"Ordinary kids," said Ben, reviewing his afternoon somewhat grimly, "don't leak memos to the Washington *Post*."

Captain Heyer had to agree. "But," he added, "unless something way out has happened, we should pick her up in a matter of hours."

"I hope you're right," said Ben, foreseeing one decision Madge and Elsie were sure to come to.

Charlie's vigil was not going to be a lonely one.

Hours later Ben was fighting a jawbreaking yawn to say:
"Look, Charlie, try to get some sleep."

In the murky darkness of suburban Maryland the porch light seemed feeble.

"You're sure you don't want to spend the night?" said Charlie blearily, although the cab was already waiting.

"No thanks. And Charlie—don't worry."

As he trudged down the path, Ben realized that he and Charlie were leaving a great deal unsaid.

It was probably just as well.

Because it was two o'clock in the morning—and the police had still found no trace of Alison Knapp.

CHAPTER 16

When the Yellow Cab finally pulled up in front of the Carlton, Ben was adding to the good resolutions he had been making all the way from Chevy Chase. Starting tomorrow, a lot of new leaves were going to be turned over. Important committee assignments or not, he was going to find time for healthful exercise—paddleboard, or a few turns in the pool. And while he was at it, there was fresh air, too. Photographers were not the only valid excuse for getting out onto a tennis court.

It was not personal vanity that turned so many congressmen into physical fitness nuts; it was the will to survive.

Ben was mentally watching himself jog religiously every morning when he awoke to find himself digging fruitlessly through his pockets.

The cabbie was looking on with open suspicion.

"Wait a minute," he said, heading for the revolving door.

But the driver knew all about hotel lobbies and side entrances. So, Ben entered the Carlton with a burly bird dog at his heels.

"Alvin," he said when the nightman at the desk looked up from *Playboy*, "I seem to have mislaid my wallet. Can you help me out?"

"Certainly, Mr. Congressman," said Alvin, who had dipped into the till for Ben before.

The taxi driver, who did not thaw until he was clutching a ten-dollar bill in his massive fist, then said, man-to-man:

"Sorry, mister, but you know how it is."

"I sure do," said Ben, wondering exactly what his subconscious meant by this.

With a chesty swagger, the driver clomped noisily to the exit, then disappeared into the night.

"Remind me to pay you back tomorrow," Ben was remarking when low voices from the elevator rank dimly penetrated his fog.

With sinking heart, he noticed Alvin's expression. Given the way things were going, this was enough to tip him off. Those were not two salesmen from Moline, over there.

"And do you want an early call tomorrow morning, Mr. Safford?" Alvin inquired punctiliously, keeping his eyes fixed on Ben.

Unfortunately, the elevators at the Carlton were not as cooperative as the staff. The two non-salesmen were still waiting when Ben finished his drawn-out instructions and reluctantly proceeded to discover what else this endless day had in store.

"Yeah, you're right, Dick. It's a big break for both of us." Congressman Herbert Adelman was humoring his companion, but his forefinger was white with pressure as he leaned on the call button. "Where *is* that damned thing? Oh, hello, Safford . . ."

"Well! If it isn't Chairman Ben Safford—of the Safford subcommittee! How are you feeling tonight, Chairman Safford? Say Herb, this calls for another round."

Dick Macnamara was still protesting that the night was young when the elevator arrived and Herb and Ben persuaded him into it.

"It's too early to break up the party," he objected.

Now that they were reasonably private, Adelman could relax. "There's always a tomorrow, Dick," he said with a grin.

Ben knew what had sparked this camaraderie. Thanks to this afternoon's disclosures, there was bound to be a lot more talk about Warren Praeger, and a lot less about these two. You could hardly blame them for wanting to celebrate.

"Tomorrow?" said Macnamara, putting out a hand to steady himself. "What good's tomorrow? Today was our big day. Tomorrow I'm going to be able to go back to work at last. You know . . ."

While Macnamara rolled on, Adelman rested in the corner, his head lolling with each lurch of the elevator.

Despite appearances Ben was not writing them off as two drunks. What he was seeing, he suspected, resulted from a couple of extra drinks on top of weeks of strain.

But even in a self-service elevator, Macnamara was talking too much. Ben could see why Adelman had hustled him out of public view.

The funereal atmosphere of a hotel corridor in the middle of the night did not get through to Macnamara, either.

". . . force the old SOB to resign," he said loudly enough to make Ben, as well as Adelman, wince. "God, Congress gets enough lousy publicity day in and day out—say, what are you fellows in such a big hurry for?"

Bed and sleep were what Ben Safford wanted. Instead, he was on the third floor of the Carlton, helping Adelman frog-march Macnamara down the endless hallway as rapidly as possible.

"For Crissake! Give it to me!" Adelman's temper was ebbing as Macnamara fumbled for a key.

Even inside, Macnamara was ready to go on.

"Can I get either of you anything to drink? Wait a minute, I don't think I brought anything with me. Well, we can call room service."

He was reaching for the phone when Ben and Adelman hastily declined. Disappointed, Macnamara ambled over to the window to stare out into the darkness.

"Dick caught me in the lobby this evening," Adelman said as if he owed Ben some explanation. "We decided to go someplace for dinner. Had a couple of drinks, then we stopped by Hogate's."

Macnamara had overheard. "I still say we should have gone on, Herb," he said.

"Sure," said Adelman. "This is just the time for you and me to be making the rounds!"

Adelman had been giving a good deal of thought to his public appearances lately. Ben would not put it past him to have stage-managed the whole evening. Being seen with Macnamara was a good way to underline the fact that Warren Praeger was currently the odd man out.

"You don't expect me to sit in a hotel room and stare at the walls, do you?" Macnamara sounded self-pitying.

Ben was beginning to wonder if he'd ever get to bed.

"Well, why are you staying here anyway?" he asked. Years of listening to domestic flack from his married colleagues had taught him one thing: hotel living, which he thought had a lot to commend it, always hit them hard.

Macnamara was no exception. He was morosely describing how much he missed Kate and the children when Adelman, who had obviously heard it all before, interrupted:

"Je-sus!" he groaned, pushing himself to his feet with a resurgence of animal energy.

With numbing earnestness, Macnamara droned on. "Of course, whenever I can get away, I go up. Then, when Congress adjourns . . ."

As a matter of principle, Ben always extended the benefit of the doubt to family men who told him how hard things were. Herb Adelman, with a young family permanently based in Brooklyn whether or not Congress was in session, could be less respectful.

"You'll get used to it," he said, breaking in on Macnamara's lament. "Unless . . ."

The switch was too abrupt for Macnamara. "Unless what?"

The younger man emitted a short bark of laughter. "We're not out of the woods, yet, you know."

Macnamara sagged into a chair. "Are you talking about the hearings?"

"What else?"

This sobered Macnamara.

"God, after all the trouble I took to avoid Shirley Knapp," he said. "I had enough sense to steer clear of her. It isn't as if I have anything to hide . . ."

Adelman frowned. "You're not saying that I do, are you?"

"No, no. But Warren Praeger sure as hell did, didn't he?"

"Nickels and dimes," Adelman said contemptuously, jerking his head toward Ben for confirmation. "Sure, now everybody knows how cheap Praeger comes. But those joyrides are small potatoes—and Safford knows it! We're talking about a fifty thousand dollar bribe! Let alone Shirley Knapp getting her brains blown out! Don't kid yourself, Dick. The rough stuff is still ahead of us!"

Without waiting for any rebuttals, he said good night.

The door had barely closed behind him when Dick Macnamara began, "Herb thinks he knows everything."

Right now, Ben admired anybody with sense enough to disengage so neatly.

"That must have been quite an outing the two of you had," he commented.

"God knows we deserved it. The last two weeks have been hell," Macnamara justified himself. "And with Warren Praeger getting taken apart . . . it's all over but the shouting, isn't it?"

Maybe it was, thought Ben, maybe not. Time would tell. Meanwhile, however, he was struck by the difference between Macnamara and Adelman. Praeger's greed made him a natural whipping boy. But there was just so much mileage to be gotten out of junkets to Acapulco. Adelman knew this; apparently Macnamara did not.

Ben avoided committing himself. "Adelman doesn't seem to think so."

"Herb's so damned busy cashing in on the whole thing," Macnamara said, "that he thinks he's the only one who can follow the ball. Just because I don't go around giving TV interviews and making grandstand plays—"

Ben had some words of wisdom. "Don't blame Adelman for trying to take care of himself," he said. "When you're under the gun, you're all alone."

"I'd be better off alone," Macnamara retorted with a humorless snort. "First, it's Herb turning the whole damn mess into a television special on behalf of Herbert Adelman. Then, it's Praeger with his sticky fingers. Talk about guilt by association! Hell, no matter what happens, I'm going to end up being a bum by association."

As Ben was willing to admit, he had a point. But the middle of the night is a bad time to submit bids for sympathy.

"Look on the bright side," he said. "You're not in jail."

"That's not funny!"

"I didn't intend it to be," said Ben, who had done too much listening for one day. "And you haven't been murdered, either.

You haven't even been cracked over the head. Your daughter hasn't disappeared . . ."

"You've lost me!" said Macnamara, who was not in the mood for counting his blessings. "What's that about a daughter?"

"Alison Knapp," Ben said. "She's missing. The police are trying to track her down. I'm just trying to remind you, Macnamara, that bad as things are—"

But Macnamara interrupted unceremoniously.

"You mean Shirley Knapp's girl?" he asked in bewilderment. "My God, what the hell is going on now? It's just one thing after another. And I thought we were coming to the end!"

With dawn fast approaching, Ben felt no more qualms about pouring cold water.

"She may have been killed," he said. "Somebody killed her mother—remember? As Adelman says, Macnamara, the rough stuff is still ahead. My advice to you is to prepare for it—by getting some sleep! At least, that's what I'm going to do!"

CHAPTER 17

Tomorrow came too soon for Ben Safford, and he didn't like the looks of it from the beginning. By the time he was on his second cup of coffee, his plans for the day had already been disrupted by a series of phone calls.

First came the news that the committee hearings were going to have to be postponed. Warren Praeger, according to his wife, had a very bad cold. Ben had barely downed the receiver after informing a sleepy Madge of the need for rearrangements before the next bulletin arrived.

Alison Knapp was alive and safe, in Captain Heyer's office.

By the time Ben got there, she was already taking on all comers.

". . . having the police hunt me down!" she stormed.

Charlie's neck was red. "What the hell did you expect me to do? You didn't even have the decency—"

Alison came surging out of her chair. "I don't have to listen to you. I can—"

Almost lazily, Captain Heyer intervened. "Sit down. You too, Congressman," he greeted Safford before reverting to Alison. "It doesn't make any difference what your father wants. The police aren't letting a key witness skip town."

Alison's eyes widened. "I'm not a witness to anything."

"Who are you trying to kid?" Heyer was scornful. "You started the whole wheel spinning. We already know how you kicked things off so your mother got murdered. Now I want to find out if Barbara Underwood's skull got fractured thanks to you."

Alison went white. "You know I didn't have anything to do with Mother being murdered," she said, sounding as if she were trying to convince herself.

Heyer did not answer her directly but addressed Charlie instead. "She's got to face facts some time. She's in this up to her neck. Either she's got something to do with two murderous assaults, or she's going to be the next body we find. This is no time to pretend we're having a tea party."

Charlie wanted some background first. "Where'd you find her?"

Heyer threw two objects onto the desk. "She was hitchhiking to New York—with a passport and a plane ticket to Amsterdam in her pocket."

Charlie nodded. "She tried getting the fare out of me the other day."

Color was flooding back to Alison's cheeks. "I don't need your money. Since you're so tight, I can get along fine without it."

"She sold her Mustang," Heyer explained. "At the big lot over near the university."

Surprise made Charlie protest. "You mean you sold your car for a ticket to Europe? What's so special about Holland, for Christ's sake?"

"Amsterdam's a pretty good place to lose yourself in the summer," Heyer remarked. "I suppose that was what she had in mind."

"It's my vacation," Alison snapped. "What I do with it is my business."

"Not any more."

Alison eyed Heyer warily and waited for him to continue.

"I had a long talk with the guy at the used car lot," he remarked. "He said you were scared stiff. Then I backtracked you. To that place on campus—the TJU Playhouse." He paused and unhurriedly began to fill a pipe.

Alison's patience ran out. "You can't fool me. Nobody at the Playhouse would give me away."

"Oh, I wouldn't say that. By and large, I was pleasantly

surprised." Without warning, Heyer's voice cracked like a whip. "What was Barbara Underwood trying to steal from you?"

Alison shied. "That was just some crazy idea the boys got from seeing her on television," she stammered.

"It was enough to start you running like a frightened rabbit," Heyer said remorselessly. "What was she after?"

"I don't know!" Alison blurted. "God, can't any of you get that through your thick heads? What's wrong with all of you? What makes you think I've got anything?"

She was shaking, and had to bite her underlip for a moment before she could continue: "Why don't you leave me alone? Why are you all picking on me?"

"You've gone to a lot of trouble to make a reputation for yourself," Heyer said gravely. "As far as the outside world is concerned, you still may have something stashed away in a drawer. Now, it doesn't matter what I think, or what your father thinks. But, if you've got a murderer thinking that way, it could mean life or death to you."

"I took one lousy little memo," she flashed back. "I gave it to the *Post* and I don't have anything else! How many times do I have to say it?"

Captain Heyer was not satisfied. He continued to bear down until she was near exhaustion. But the essentials of Alison Knapp's story never altered.

"All right," he said at last. "Go wash your face. Then, you can sign the statement they're typing up."

After she left, he turned to Charlie. "Well, Mr. Knapp, you wanted your daughter back. Now, you've got her."

Charlie was in no mood for sarcasm. "To hell with that. Clue me in about Mrs. Underwood."

"There's a lot I don't know," Heyer replied. "But I'll tell you what I picked up from a couple of the kids down at the Playhouse. One of them named Jerry told me about a telephone call Alison got from the NPA over a week ago. It seems that Carrington wanted any documents belonging to her mother."

Ben reacted faster than Charlie. "Now wait a minute," he interrupted. "You mean that Alison really is hanging onto something of Shirley's?"

"This isn't exactly firsthand, you know," Heyer replied. "Alison told the kids at the Playhouse what Carrington wanted. I suppose she was trying to make herself interesting. Anyway, she wouldn't say outright whether or not she had anything."

Charlie groaned. "That's all we need. Alison hinting that she's got some of Shirley's files."

"Wait until you hear the next bit." Heyer sounded worried. "Last week a woman showed up at TJU when Alison wasn't there. She said she was from the *Post* and authorized to collect whatever papers Alison was keeping at the Playhouse. A boy called Pete had a hard time getting rid of her. That got Alison bragging about being in demand at the *Post*. But Pete's not stupid, not by a long shot. He told her it was dangerous to keep shooting off her mouth. I guess he got through to her because that's when she started talking about going to Europe. Well, you can guess what happened next."

Ben could. "Pete saw the picture of Mrs. Underwood on television?"

"Right as rain. Of course, what he should have done was come down here and tell us. Instead he told Alison that it was Mrs. Underwood who'd been nosing around the Playhouse. He tried to persuade her to come to the police."

"So that's why she lit out," Charlie supplied the conclusion himself.

"Yes. She sold her car, bought her ticket and started thumbing her way to New York. She was picked up in Pennsylvania." Heyer spread his hands in a gesture of defeat. "And it's still a toss-up whether she was bolting because she had something, or because people thought she had. You both heard her story. Your guess is as good as mine."

Ben did not pretend to be an expert on nineteen-year-old girls. "I don't think we'll get anywhere trying to figure out Alison. But what about Carrington? You said he called her, Captain."

Heyer shook his head. "Not exactly. Jerry answered the phone, and he says it was a woman who called from the NPA. Carrington's going to be able to claim that this was just another one of Barbara Underwood's independent operations."

Ben raised an objection. "What do you mean—*another*? With

Mrs. Underwood in a coma, we've only got Carrington's word that she wasn't following his orders all the time."

"The police don't take anybody's word for anything, Mr. Congressman. We look at what people do. Now Carrington knows a lot he hasn't told us. But Mrs. Underwood was playing it by ear. She looked in so many places and tried so many dodges, she couldn't have known a damn thing. Hell, she didn't even know for sure that there was a document."

"Neither do we," said Ben.

Heyer agreed. "That's right. There are three possibilities. Either the murderer himself has the document, or somebody else has it, or there isn't any document."

It took Charlie a while to calculate the odds. "If the murderer has it, that's okay," he said slowly.

"From your point of view, maybe," Heyer grunted. "Not from mine."

"When you say somebody else, you mean Alison, don't you?"

"She's the logical one. I doubt if anybody else is crazy enough to fool with that kind of dynamite."

"I think I see what you're getting at," Charlie said. "The murderer can't be absolutely sure there isn't any document—not the way Shirley was starting to write things down. If he's gotten hold of it, he's safe. But otherwise, sooner or later, he's going to begin wondering if Alison has it."

"That's right." Heyer knew there was more coming.

"Goddammit!" Charlie roared in anger. "You're using her as bait, that's what you're doing."

"I don't use young girls as bait, Mr. Knapp. I haven't done a damn thing."

"You could have let Alison go to Europe," Charlie said stubbornly.

"And have all this kick up again when she comes back? Use your head, Mr. Knapp. I'll assign a couple of men to Alison now, but I can't hand out police protection forever."

Charlie sank back. "Maybe the murderer got what he wanted off Mrs. Underwood."

"I wouldn't want to kid you, Mr. Knapp. The murderer was scared off before he finished that job. There wasn't any time for him to search her."

Charlie looked at Ben. "What in God's name am I supposed to do now?"

"I think the captain is suggesting you put yourself in his hands," Ben said.

"And wait for someone to murder Alison too?" Charlie took a deep breath. "Like hell I will!"

CHAPTER 18

By the time Captain Heyer was willing to call it a day, he was disgruntled, Charlie was steaming and Ben was tired of being their buffer.

"That isn't doing any good," he said, interrupting a tirade as he and Charlie took the stairs down to the stenographic room.

Charlie halted at the turn, blocking their progress. His hand was kneading the knob of the railing as if he yearned to do violence to something.

"Then what will?" he challenged.

"There's only one way you can protect Alison. Make sure she isn't holding anything back."

"Oh, I'll do that," Charlie said perfunctorily.

"If she is, then yank it out of her and deliver it to Heyer. He'll spread the news so nobody will have anything to gain by silencing Alison." Ben came to a full stop.

Charlie would not let it rest there. "That's fine and dandy, Ben, assuming she's got something. But what if she doesn't?"

"Then you're stuck," Ben said sadly.

"For Christ's sake, that doesn't make sense!" Charlie exploded. "She's even less of a threat that way. And you're telling me that she's in more danger."

Ben knew better than to say the danger was largely of her own making. "She may be less of a threat, but how's the murderer to know that? You can't explain it to him when you don't know who he is."

"I don't know if I go along with you." Charlie sounded thoughtful as he turned for the last half flight. "But I'll give you this much. The first thing is to handle Alison."

"Well, you can do that better without me. Anyway, I've got to get back to work," said Ben.

Charlie had not been listening. "I'm almost sure that's going to be a washout. Then I guess I'll have to start talking turkey to somebody else."

Two hours later Charlie was on phase two of his program.

"I'm so sorry," said the receptionist, "but Mr. Carrington is very busy. If you would like to make an appointment . . . ?"

She was everything the receptionist for a powerful trade association should be—beautiful, ladylike, and efficient. Her voice conveyed overpowering sympathy and helpfulness.

Charlie ignored it all.

"He'll see me. Tell him I'm Shirley's husband."

For an instant the receptionist became human.

"Her husband?" she repeated blankly. Then she lowered her head over the intercom.

Within minutes Charlie was entering the office of the NPA's president. There he wasted no time.

"I understand you're Shirley's executor, Mr. Knapp," John Carrington began formally. "I suppose you've come about her pension plan."

"No. I've come about her murder."

For a moment they silently appraised each other.

So this is what Shirley ended up with, thought Charlie, absorbing the smooth expensive room and the smooth expensive man before him.

So this is what Shirley started out with, thought Carrington, looking at Charlie.

"I don't see how I can help you there," Carrington said carefully. He already suspected that Charlie spelled trouble.

"You're the only one who can. This whole ball-up started because Shirley bribed someone for the NPA. Then when things got rough, she was murdered so she couldn't talk."

"Now wait a minute. I haven't—"

Charlie was not giving Carrington a chance to deny anything. Ruthlessly he proceeded.

"That's bad enough. But I wasn't taking care of Shirley. I am taking care of Alison. And I'm not sitting back while she has her brains blown out, too."

"Alison?" Carrington recovered almost at once. "Oh, the daughter."

"She's not on your payroll. She's not getting a salary to play target for some maniac the NPA is greasing."

Carrington flushed. "Even making allowance for your feelings, Knapp, I don't see how this helps."

"Alison is only nineteen years old. I want her to live to be twenty."

"All right! You don't have to tell me this man is dangerous. I've seen his handiwork, right on my doorstep."

"I know," Charlie said heavily.

"What's that supposed to mean?" Carrington asked between clenched teeth.

"What was Mrs. Underwood up to?"

"I'll be damned if I know."

"She worked for you, didn't she?" Charlie insisted.

"I'm beginning to wonder."

"Was she trying on blackmail?"

Carrington met his eyes. "If she was, she was doing it on her own hook."

"Even so, she had to know who to work on." Charlie was beginning to zero in. "She not only had to have something to sell, she had to have someone to sell it to."

"Look, maybe you know what you're talking about. I don't."

"Alison stole a memo. Now the word's gone out that there may be another one. Is that what Mrs. Underwood was peddling?"

"How should I know?"

"Don't give me that, Carrington." Charlie was steely. "You know what Shirley wrote to you. Sure, I've heard all about your shredding machines, but they don't work on your memory, do they? I'm asking you flat out, did you ever get anything from Shirley that could have left a carbon floating around? Now, I'm not some congressional committee. It can't do any harm to tell me. But I mean to find out."

Carrington did not answer immediately, but considered his unexpected visitor. Then, when he had made up his mind, he sighed.

"All right. I'll tell you and a lot of good it will do you. The same idea occurred to me. When that first memo appeared in the *Post*, I thought Shirley had gotten sloppy about security. Now I don't think so any more. I'd be willing to bet no incriminating carbons ever got to this office. Shirley kept them at home until the original had gone through, then she destroyed them. That's how your girl got her hands on one. But Mrs. Underwood never had a chance. And here's something else. Shirley wrote that one memo —and that's all."

"So you say there isn't anything?"

"I said there wasn't any interoffice memo. If Shirley tried to safeguard herself at the last minute, that's a different kettle of fish. For all I know, she could have put something in her safe deposit box."

But Charlie knew better. "No, Shirley was killed at the airport. She never went home or anywhere else in Washington. That proves Alison didn't have a chance to get her hands on any last minute effort."

"You've overlooked one thing," Carrington said softly. "That last week Shirley wasn't seeing her daughter—only her husband."

Charlie brushed this aside. "I'm not the one in danger. It's Alison. Which brings me to my next point. Shirley wasn't a deaf mute. She talked plenty. She could have told Mrs. Underwood who she bribed."

"If you mean Shirley told her outright, no. She might have dropped clues."

"And not only to Mrs. Underwood."

Carrington smiled wearily. "You're asking me if I know. Well, I don't."

"Carrington, you can't hide behind Shirley now that she's dead. You'd like to pretend this was something between Shirley and her bought congressman and that you didn't have anything to do with it. But there's fifty thousand dollars tying you into it."

Carrington was sure of himself. "So I'm tied in. That doesn't mean I know who the money went to."

"For God's sake!" Charlie roared. "Don't you see what I'm after? The only way I can take care of Alison is if I know who I'm protecting her against. I'm not asking you for proof."

"I don't have proof."

"Forget proof. Just tell me about those little clues Shirley dropped."

"I'm sorry." Carrington shook his head regretfully. "You're barking up the wrong tree. Mrs. Underwood knew when Shirley went out and sometimes even where she went. She could have picked up a lot. But I was two thousand miles away."

"Shelling out fifty thousand bucks on Shirley's say-so," Charlie scoffed.

He was getting under Carrington's skin.

"If you use your head, you'll realize Shirley was my insulation."

"From where I sit, it looks as if she was your fall guy."

This outraged Carrington. "You've got no call to say that! Hell, congressmen have been bribed before. They didn't turn around and start shooting everyone in sight."

Charlie tried a new tack.

"This Underwood woman. If she knew anything, she might have told someone. Have you thought of that?"

Carrington did not hide his dislike. "I've talked to her husband," he said. "According to him, Barbara Underwood just put in her hours here."

Charlie was contemptuous. "That's a great line after she's been bashed on the head while she was running around Washington in a lot of disguises."

"He doesn't notice much." Carrington glared at Charlie. "I'm not responsible for the men my employees marry."

It took Charlie a moment to put two and two together. Then he grinned. "If you don't want me around your neck, it's easy enough to get rid of me. Just name the guy you bribed."

"I'm telling you for the last time I don't know. And I'm beginning to wonder what your game is."

Charlie was dead serious. "I don't have any game. I'm simply trying to protect my daughter."

"You're choosing a damned funny way to do it. Why don't you go to the police?"

"I've been."

Carrington was becoming speculative. "You say you're worried about your daughter. But I'm not forgetting that Shirley ran to you when she was on the spot. God knows why! But the person she saw during her last week was you. If she put anything down on paper, you're the one who'd be holding it."

"Oh, for Christ's sake." Charlie made one last try. "Shirley didn't give me anything."

John Bowie Carrington did not believe him.

Charlie was discouraged when he left the NPA.

"These people are so damned cute they'd zigzag to get the morning paper," he told himself. "And if I make the rounds of these three congressmen, it'll be the same all over. The more you talk about something not existing, the more you convince people that it does."

He was halfway down the street before he realized what this meant. Heedless of the grumbling crowd, he stopped in his tracks.

"That's it!" he murmured, plunging his hand into his pocket. His finger began fumbling through the fistful of change.

What Charlie Knapp wanted now was a nice private telephone booth.

CHAPTER 19

Ben got back to his office to find that he had been in demand.

"Mr. Cargill, and Mr. Winley called." Madge had barely begun her list when the light on Ben's phone blinked.

Taking chances recklessly, he answered himself.

"Ben!" said Janet from Newburg. "Where on earth have you been? I tried getting you last night. Then this morning, Madge said you had called off the hearing but she didn't know where you were."

"As a matter of fact," Ben included Madge in his explanation, "I had to go down to the police station. They picked up Alison Knapp."

"What?"

Both Janet and Madge were barraging him with questions when a raucous clamor drowned them out.

"For God's sake, there goes the buzzer," said Ben. "Why are we having a quorum call at this time of day? Janet, I've got to go. Madge can fill you in . . ."

Thrusting the receiver at Madge, he set forth on the double. When he found himself huffing and puffing alongside John Cargill (R-Vt.), he repeated himself.

"Goddam foolishness," Cargill said uninformatively.

"I'll bet," said Ben. "But what's the emergency?"

It was the House's annual twenty-four-hour spring madness, which had been somewhat delayed this year. Ben, Cargill, and every other congressman available, were trying to muster a quorum in order to repeal a bill, passed late the night before, which terminated all foreign aid and civil service pay.

"I don't know which is worse," Cargill finished dourly. "Dodoes who sneak here in the middle of the night and start baying at the moon—or people like you, who don't sit still for a minute. Tried getting you last night! Tried getting you this morning!"

Ben did not like hearing himself bracketed with the House's delinquents.

"Well, I'm here now, ready to vote on the side of the angels," he said, deciding to skip the police station. Cargill's sympathies were not wide. "Anyway, I thought you were all for economy in government, John."

The light touch is not what Vermont seeks in its elected officials. Cargill greeted Ben's mild attempt with a stony face and said: "After we've taken care of this loonyness, I want ten minutes of your time—"

"Ben!" The bottleneck in the Lobby funneled Ben right into Milo Winley. "Where've you been! I've been looking high and low for you."

"There'll be a short wait for a table," said Ben.

Winley did not let this deflect him. "Listen, we've got to get together about that Irrigation Bill revision. Once we're finished here—"

Cargill tightened his grip on Ben's forearm.

"Later this afternoon, Milo," said Ben, backed up by a predatory stare from Cargill.

Winley was being borne off by the tide. "Well, don't wait too long. And Ben, believe me, it's damned inconvenient when your girl keeps saying she doesn't know . . ."

The rest of his complaint was swallowed in the general din.

"You can unhand me now," Ben said since Cargill showed an inclination to cling to him like a leech.

"I just don't want you chasing off," Cargill replied, complying in time to let Elsie Hollenbach interpose herself.

"Ben," she said, inclining her head toward Cargill, "what's happened about Alison? Madge has been telling me that she didn't know where you were. Naturally, I've been eager to hear all about it."

"Hmph!" said Cargill.

It took more than Yankee cantankerousness to subdue Mrs. Hollenbach. "Unless you're careful, John, you're going to be counted absent. I believe they're getting close to the C's. Now then . . ."

Ben was describing a tearful Alison when Elsie too had to leave.

"Of course, I'm happy that the girl is safe," she said in parting. "Although this suggestion that there may be revelations to come troubles me. Perhaps we should think about subpoenaing Alison Knapp for the hearings . . ."

"That's right," said Cargill returning. "You're chairing that subcommittee, aren't you?"

A workhorse himself, he respected any strong back among his colleagues.

"I sure am," said Ben with feeling. "But right now the S's are coming up. Those voting machines are going to be a big step forward around here."

With this thrust at tradition, he ducked onto the Floor in time to do his part in saving the Republic.

When he got back to the Lobby, he found that Cargill was mellowed.

"What was that you were telling Elsie about the police, eh? Come up with something, have you?"

The whole House of Representatives had a real interest in the Ad Hoc Committee, and the police, these days. Even Cargill was not immune.

Ben disabused him.

"I see." Cargill was disappointed. "You notice that Adelman's the only one here to vote today? I don't say he's one of my favorites but—"

"Praeger has a cold," said Ben. "Macnamara missed a roll call, the way all of us—except Elsie—do. Quit pumping, John. What is it you want to see me about?"

Cargill expounded all the way back to Ben's office. It concerned his own peculiar specialty. Congressman Cargill was a hybrid, watchdog as well as workhorse. He put in long hours nosing out bureaucratic bungles. To date, his peak was forty-seven thousand butter knives stockpiled by a U. S. Air Force installation near Bremerhaven.

"But this one's a beaut, too," he said, producing a familiarly sober GPO publication and brandishing it at Ben. "You know what Indian Affairs have done? They've released this study."

In co-operation with several universities, the Bureau of Indian Affairs had just concluded a two-year experiment involving cash grants to low-income families in selected southwest counties.

"Just handed over the money!" Cargill talked them right past Madge who, to judge from her open mouth, also had something to say.

"No Indians left in Vermont, huh?" Ben replied, nodding to let Madge know he was going to cut this as short as he could.

"So, I sat right down and read it," Cargill continued. "You know what the Bureau found out, Ben? When you give people money, they spend it. How do you like that! Some of these Indians took their two or three thousand dollars and put it into TV sets or cars. Some of them did work on their houses. Some of them settled their back bills. Now, Ben, I ask you! Is that what we pay taxes for?"

Ben almost fell into the abyss before he realized that this time Cargill was not gunning for the underprivileged.

"What do they suppose people do with money?" Cargill demanded irately. "This bunch of big thinkers from universities—several universities, mind you—don't know enough to wipe themselves. Experiments to see what people do with money! Hell, why pay sociologists fat salaries to find that out? Any ten-year-old kid could tell you. Now Ben, we've got a responsibility to keep these geniuses from throwing away tax money on this kind of horse water."

Cargill had not only identified the problem, he saw how to solve it.

"I want us to find out how many sociologists there are on the federal payroll, and kick them off!"

On issues that separated the men from the boys, Ben was always willing to stand and be counted.

"Good," said Cargill now satisfied. "You know what? I feel sorry for those poor damn Indians!"

It was the thin end of the wedge. Congress, like life, was endlessly unexpected, Ben mused. Who would have thought that a few Navahos would succeed where so many others had failed?

Madge was lying in wait even before Cargill cleared the door, eager to take up where she had left off.

"Mr. Cargill," she began again. "I guess you've taken care of him, haven't you?"

"I guess so, Madge," Ben replied with a grin. "He thinks we don't need Ph.D.'s to tell us what people do when you give them money. They spend it."

". . . and Mr. Winley," said Madge severely.

"I've got him set up later today."

". . . and Mr. Bullivant. Then, General Trainer wants you to call back. And I told the Crop Outlook people you'd send them that letter . . ."

Madge had been planning to drive her message home by heaping instance on instance. But she was just warming up when she shot a look at Ben and then broke off.

He was not listening.

"And the Ohio Development Commission called," she said with special emphasis.

"Mm," said Ben, unconsciously drawing Indian war bonnets on the pad before him. "A lot of important people wanted to get in touch with me this morning, didn't they? And I wasn't available. Makes you think, doesn't it?"

Whatever this meant, Madge knew it was not contrition.

To all appearances, Ben was completely intent on his pencil, still embellishing feathered regalia. But when he finally looked up, he had made his decision.

"Madge, do me a favor, will you? Call Heyer and see if he can spare me a couple of minutes. Just say that a few things have come up that I want to tell him about."

Madge then showed her stuff. Without so much as a raised eyebrow, she got back to her desk. Five minutes later she had a report.

"Captain Heyer's not at headquarters," she said. "He's over at Georgetown Hospital. That's where Mrs. Underwood . . ."

But Ben was already making for the door. "I think I'd better try catching him there!"

Hospital waiting rooms are always cheerless. Despite all efforts, anxiety and tension outweigh comfortable chairs and soothing color schemes. The paging system, with its endless droning and the white-clad doctors and nurses who hurry past are unwelcome reminders of what lies beyond the swinging doors.

Ben had to wait ten minutes for Captain Heyer.

"Mr. Congressman," he said, "they told me you wanted to see me."

Ben was well aware that they had parted company only a few hours earlier, so he plunged right in:

"Maybe I'm wasting your time," he said. "But I've had a couple of ideas."

Heyer sat down. "Let's hear them," he invited. Then, laying his own cards on the table, he added: "Ideas are what I'm fresh out of. You were there this morning. You know we're up a tree, until someone makes a move on that Knapp girl."

Ben could not keep from glancing in the general direction of the wards and private rooms. Captain Heyer would not be in Georgetown Hospital if Mrs. Barbara Underwood were still unconscious.

"She's come around but she isn't much help," Heyer told him. "She claims she doesn't remember a thing, not even who hit her. And she's still too weak for real questioning. So, anything you've got to say . . ."

Ben took a deep breath and began: "Today, I caught a lie we all missed. And that flushed something else. We've all been using the wrong starting point."

Despite the fatigue lines etching his face, Captain Heyer was still functioning. "Today? You mean something from Alison Knapp that I overlooked? Or did she open up later, once you all left?"

"No," said Ben quickly. "The Knapps went their way and I headed back to the Hill. That's where I saw daylight."

A hopeful stir from his companion made him add a cautionary note: "Not that I got anything from the horse's mouth. As a matter of fact, Herb Adelman was the only one there. Neither Praeger nor Macnamara showed up."

Heyer dug out his tobacco pouch. "Okay," he said, abandoning wishful thinking about sensational disclosures in the Speaker's Lobby. "You said something about a starting point. Alison Knapp swipes that memo from her mother's desk and gives it to the *Post*—"

Once again, Ben called a halt. "No, that's when the whistle blew. The kickoff came months ago, when Shirley Knapp bribed a congressman to kill Section C. After that—well, you know what politicians say. Take a look at the record."

He had done just that this afternoon while Madge looked on. And it was as damning as Shirley Knapp's famous memo. There were video tapes, and transcripts of official statements. There was even testimony given under oath.

"And somewhere, God knows where, there have to be receipted bills," Ben finished, recalling John Cargill's Indians. "Those, I think we can take on faith. We've been looking through the wrong end of the telescope. The motive for killing Shirley Knapp was clear enough, but it applies too many people. What happened while Mrs. Knapp was still alive is what tells the story . . ."

By the time he finished, Heyer was sold. "What you say hangs together, all right. And it does spotlight one man, instead of a bunch. But where does that leave us?"

Ben had seen this one coming. John Cargill, among others, had nudged him from one jarring discrepancy toward one enduring truth. But he had been a lawyer before he had been a congressman.

"Not enough evidence for a jury," he agreed.

There was more frustration than phlegm in Heyer's throat clearing.

"I should have spotted that phone call myself," he said. "But how much good will it do us anyway? Everybody had plenty of opportunity to kill Mrs. Knapp. And the courts—"

He broke off so bitterly that Ben hesitated in making his next comment. "It may take a while but we'll nail him on the bribery. And once we've done that—"

"Bribery, hell! I want this baby for murder." Heyer pushed himself up from the sofa with massive disgust. "Well, I suppose we'd better get going. You want a lift?"

They were almost at the exit when the revolving door produced a familiar figure.

"Charlie! What are you doing here?" Ben exclaimed, then did a double-take.

Two uniformed policemen were propelling Charlie forward. "I came back to tell the cops what I've done," he said defiantly. One of the men flanking him whistled aloud.

"Boy, did you! Captain, wait until you hear what this guy's been up to! You won't believe it!"

CHAPTER 20

By the time they all adjourned to the sidewalk in front of Georgetown Hospital, the sky was an ominous, liverish yellow. Dulled by distance, thunder rumbled on the horizon.

Standing by the squad car, Captain Heyer played the door back and forth in a controlled three-inch arc.

". . . this goddammed Mickey Mouse operation of yours, Knapp," he said thickly. "Sure you tried to make each one think he was the only one you were putting the bite on. But what if they get together?"

Charlie was unconcerned. "Ben's already said he'll take care of that," he replied. "Why don't you stop bitching? I set things up so you can catch a murderer in the act."

"Like hell! I ought—"

Heyer was really punishing the hinges when Ben Safford intervened.

"Don't push your luck, Charlie. You've handed Heyer a chance to get what he needs, which is a little hard proof. But if this is going to work, we'd all better get moving."

Heyer let the door swing open. "Yeah," he said, "we're going to have the whole damned zoo staked out. But I'm still worried . . ."

Ben already had his assignment. He was shoving Charlie toward the taxi stand when Captain Heyer's final comment reached them.

"Good luck! You're gonna need it."

"What we have to do, Madge," said Ben urgently, "is to make sure that people don't get a chance to check notes on what Charlie said to them. All three of them know that he's going to be at the Zoo at quarter to eight tonight. Between now and then"—it was slightly after four—"we've got to do our damnedest to keep a clear field, so the murderer swallows the bait."

While Madge started dialing, Charlie Knapp reported from the window. "Raining now. Pretty hard."

"Great," said Ben. "That's all we need—low visibility . . . Oh, Elsie? Listen, I have a favor to ask you . . ."

With time running out, Ben's explanations were necessarily truncated.

But, to his enormous relief, everybody from Val Oakes to Tony Martinelli, was ready to improvise.

"Sure I understand," said Tony, who took in complexities with Machiavellian zest. "But you're betting somebody's real dumb, aren't you?"

"Not dumb—desperate," Ben said.

"Maybe," said Tony. Then he went on: "You think your friend Knapp realizes he's got some guy coming after him with a gun?"

Ben looked toward Charlie who was stolidly inspecting a wall map. "He knows, all right."

"I think we've taken care of everything," Madge announced when Ben sank back after the last telephone call. "Now it's just a question of waiting—"

"And praying," said Charlie Knapp cheerfully.

Not bad, thought Ben Safford, for a man inviting a murderer to kill him.

". . . and meat loaf. I'll mash some potatoes to go with . . ." Still addressing the living room, Mildred Praeger bustled to answer the door. "Why . . ."

"Good evening, Mrs. Praeger," said Elsie Hollenbach, ignoring the dismayed confusion. "I understand Warren isn't feeling well."

She advanced with unassailable assurance, making it impossible for Mrs. Praeger to do anything but respond conventionally.

"How nice . . . Warren gets so bored . . . only a cold, but you know how miserable . . . Warren! Look who's dropped by!"

Her distracted burblings carried them from the hallway to the living room. There, Warren Praeger's initial astonishment dissolved immediately.

"Let me assure you, Mrs. Hollenbach," he said self-righteously, "that as soon as I am able, I shall meet the committee—"

His sudden, frame-racking sneeze elicited maternal clucking from Mildred. While she rushed over to renew his supply of Kleenex, Elsie composedly sat and waited for the fuss to die down.

"I am not the committee's truant officer," she finally said with some truth. "Although it would be foolish to claim that this is a simple social call."

Elsie Hollenbach was the Voice of Conscience in the House; she was a luminary in Praeger's party. That, she and Ben had agreed, made her a natural to tackle him.

She was also a past master at playing things by ear.

"Yes?" Praeger said with reluctant interest.

On the sofa beside him, Mildred folded her plump hands and watched Mrs. Hollenbach anxiously. "I've never known anybody who gets hit harder by colds," she said emphatically. "Every year we go through this."

Praeger seemed willing to let appearances speak for themselves. His reddened nose and streaming eyes were supported by nasal sprays and crumpled tissues. But what really convinced Elsie was the bathrobe, Praeger's thin white ankles, and the bedroom slippers.

". . . if you feel well enough to discuss it now," she said. "I have been considering the impact of these hearings on the elections. Some sort of group action is called for . . ."

Like the practiced speaker she was, Elsie savored audience reaction as she spoke. On the face of it, Mildred was easy. She wanted, heart and soul, to believe that there was hope. But Praeger was a tougher nut to crack. Warily he sat measuring everything Elsie said against the sting of her questions yesterday.

"I agree that the hearings will be an issue in the elections," he said with renewed resentment. "Now, you say you have something to propose?"

Behind the brusqueness, there was a guarded flicker.

"Under the circumstances, I think we should co-opt the National

Committee," Elsie said, confining herself to generalities yet implying everything.

"That has interesting possibilities," he said dubiously enough to let her spin her thread out.

"Frankly, Warren, a show of party unity would be of inestimable assistance to you particularly," she said with her customary directness.

She was not destined to know Warren Praeger's reaction.

"Oh my goodness!" Mildred cried. "Warren, look at the time. You've got to start getting dressed!"

Praeger obediently jumped to his feet, sketched excuses to his guest and hustled out of the room.

"Warren has an appointment with the doctor in fifteen minutes," Mildred said firmly. "Dr. Brauer is fitting him in. So, I'm afraid . . ."

Mrs. Hollenbach had no alternative.

"Tell Warren I'll discuss this with him later," she said, noticing that Mildred Praeger was leading her to the door, not following. "And I hope he feels better."

"Oh, I will, I will," said Mrs. Praeger absently. "So nice of you to visit."

But the door closed behind Mrs. Hollenbach a shade too quickly.

She was frowning when she got to the lobby but it was instinct that made her seek out a chair in the corner. Praeger certainly did have a cold, and there was no reason to doubt that he was going to the doctor. Still, Elsie would feel easier if she saw it all with her own eyes.

For ten minutes, she sat perfectly still. Then, she uncrossed her ankles, leaned back like a woman resting and took stock.

Warren should have been scurrying through the lobby by now.

Ten more minutes passed.

Elsie opened her capacious bag and started going through it. Then, clicking the clasp shut, she rose and returned to the elevator. Excuses did not bother her a bit. When the time came, she would plead gloves left behind, or a glasses case. The important thing was to be absolutely sure . . .

For the second time that afternoon, she knocked on the door of the Praeger apartment. Once, then twice.

With a chill of foreboding, Elsie checked her watch.

"Six-thirty," she said aloud. In the empty hallway, silence mocked her.

"If you want my opinion, there's nobody up there to hear you," said Val Oakes. "It's nearly six-thirty, and there aren't many people hanging around the House."

Dick Macnamara was red-faced from fifteen minutes of bellowing. "I'm afraid you're right. But we've got to get out of here." He looked around angrily, then let loose again: "Hey, up there! We're stuck! Get us some help."

Oakes exchanged glances with Lou Flecker while Macnamara stopped shouting and began a tattoo on the wall.

"Trapped in an elevator with the alarm bell not working," Lou said, when Macnamara subsided. "I'm sending a complaint direct to the Architect."

Macnamara did not comment but the elevator operator did.

"Don't know what's gone wrong," he said again.

Macnamara was doggedly fair. "It's not your fault, Wiley," he said. "This equipment must be a hundred years old. Hey, up there! Hey!"

Val Oakes underlined this reassurance by swiveling a cautious three-quarters toward Wiley and letting his right eyelid droop in a deliberate wink.

"How much longer are we going to have to stay here?" No actor, Flecker sounded more complacent than vexed.

Oakes was about to weigh in when he heard something even less satisfactory.

"Listen!" said Macnamara unnecessarily. "They've heard us. They're trying!" He expelled a heartfelt breath of relief. "We may even get out of here in time."

A distinct tremor in the elevator testified to rescue attempts.

"I wonder what went wrong," Macnamara said without much interest.

Congressmen Flecker and Oakes, as well as old Wiley, could have told him. Ben Safford's hurried briefing had left details to Val and Lou. When these old swamp foxes compared notes, they agreed that it was tempting providence not to use the materials at hand.

"We could call a committee meeting. Or, hell, we could set up an appointment with the Attorney-General. He'd go along," Flecker had said, canvassing the advantages of rank.

Val Oakes reviewed homelier possibilities. "Or we could get someone to accidentally lock him in his office," he had said, running down the House staff from Doorkeeper to Chaplain. "But he's got his own keys."

From there, it had been no effort to get to Wiley, the elevator, and a carefully instructed cast.

"No use breaking our backs," Val had said as he and Lou set out to corral Macnamara. "We get him into the elevator with us, and from there on, other people take over."

Up to now everything, including the shuddering halt between floors, had gone like clockwork. But Wiley's rolling eyes told their own story even before the elevator hiccupped, then resumed its ascent.

"Not so bad after all," said Dick Macnamara.

"No," said Val Oakes heavily. "No, it wasn't."

The fresh young face responsible for this premature release was not the only unwelcome sight to greet them. Reporters were streaming out of a late session of the Foreign Affairs Committee. They fell on Three Congressmen Trapped in House Elevator.

"So, you were there for fifteen minutes! Tell us how . . ."

"Are you going to insist on an inquiry?"

Oakes tried to disentangle himself, but his bulk was against him. Macnamara cut through the crowd with a firm athletic stride and disappeared from view.

"And short of hog-tying him," Val summed up minutes later, "there wasn't a thing we could do. Hell, I thought this was going to work right."

Lou Flecker was still hoping. "Maybe it was enough."

"It wasn't," said Val, producing a venerable Elgin. "Quarter to seven," he discovered. "And this thing's kept good time for more than thirty years!"

"No," Lou agreed, looking down the deserted hall bleakly. "No, it wasn't enough—not by a long shot."

Congressman Martinelli's timepiece was an electronic marvel.

"Damned thing's running fast," he said.

"The car clock says quarter to seven. My watch does, too. What makes you think you're running fast?" Herb Adelman was growing restive. "I have to get back to town."

"We've got plenty of time," Tony murmured as he gazed out the window of the maroon Cadillac that his administrative assistant was tooling down the rain-splashed parkway.

"We're only at Hyattsville," Adelman complained. "Can't he go any faster?"

Tony answered with a gesture toward the snail track of headlights piercing the half darkness.

Adelman bit hard to keep from saying more.

Because, for all he knew, Martinelli would still introduce him to that wealthy industrialist who contributed to the campaigns of liberal Democrats.

"No funny money," he had said abrasively when Martinelli caught him storming out of his office.

Tony swallowed hard. "Max Ruben?" he said reprovingly.

Ruben was not only an eminent art collector, he was clean as a whistle. "Max," Tony had lied like a trooper, "is down here in Baltimore on a business trip. He's an old, old friend of mine. I was telling him just the other day how much this Knapp mess is going to make you bleed."

"So?"

"And what a shame it would be if you lost your seat. So Max said he'd be glad to talk to you. But Adelman, he's a busy man. First thing tomorrow, he's flying off to London. Between you and me"—Tony embodied big city savvy—"missing him would be the biggest mistake you've ever made."

Adelman had run a hand through unruly hair. "God, any kind of contribution," he said, almost to himself.

Tony studied his opal-and-gold cuff link. "It's up to you. If we run right over to Baltimore now . . ."

Snaring Adelman had been the ticklish part. Everything else had been child's play.

First, there was the desk clerk. Mr. Ruben, he said convincingly, had been unexpectedly called away. Then there was the unaccountable difficulty in retrieving the Cadillac. Finally, this supercautious return as far as Hyattsville.

"Christ!" said Adelman aggressively. "The traffic's thinning out. Why the hell are we doing thirty-five?"

"Yeah," said Tony. "Maybe you'd better pick it up, Nick."

Nick accelerated with a rush that flattened Adelman and Martinelli against the rear cushions. Not that this worried Tony. Nick had his instructions too. That needle would be back down to forty as soon as possible.

Just then, he got some outside help. There was a soft plop. The heavy car veered dangerously close to the median strip before Nick's powerful shoulders wrestled it back to dead center, then to the breakdown lane.

"A flat," he said, as they thumped to a lopsided halt.

Adelman was swearing under his breath.

"That's the way the ball bounces," said Tony, reaching for a cigarette. "No, Nick can change it. Why get wet?"

But Adelman was too taut to sit still. Turning up his jacket collar, he hauled himself out to supervise Nick and to release tension by prowling up and down, heedless of the traffic streaming past.

Suddenly there was a scream of brakes, then voices too indistinct for Tony to follow. He was just taking notice, when the door opened.

"He hitched a ride," Nick said helplessly. "They stopped to see if they could do anything. And Adelman"—he choked on the name—"Adelman says no, but are they going to the District. Before I knew it, he cut out!"

"My God, what time is it?"

Both his Accutron and the dashboard showed 7:15.

While Tony stared venomously at the clock, Nick delivered the clincher:

"The way they took off, they'll be back in Washington in ten minutes!"

Nick was still cursing the jack at seven-thirty, precisely when Charlie Knapp nosed his Avis Chevrolet into a No PARKING spot on Cathedral Road. Pocketing the keys, he methodically collected the oversize manila envelope from the seat beside him, and set off.

Checking the time would have been like counting his fingers.

In minutes, he was going to walk through the gates and into the Zoo.

Every year, three million people did this, to saunter along tree-shaded paths, to hang over bridges and gaze down at Rock Creek, to wonder at penguins, zebras, and llamas. Charlie had hit on it by trying to think like a murderer. There are many entrances and exits to Washington's National Zoological Park.

The one he wanted was just up Connecticut Avenue.

Driving right into the Zoo would have speeded up action considerably. But the choreographer takes his beat from the music. It might be a macabre duet, but somewhere on this soggy, leaden evening, another man was heading for the Zoo. And he, too, was on foot. He would not be flaunting a license plate—not on this mission.

Maximum exposure, you could call it, Charlie reflected as he trudged through the steady drizzle. Thanks to Ben Safford's insistence, he wore a last-minute purchase. But the cheap drugstore plastic raincoat was not much protection or disguise.

Bareheaded and deliberate, Charlie walked on.

He attracted little attention from the outbound flow leaving the Zoo just before closing time. A few families shepherding children ahead of them were fleetingly curious about this lonely figure. Then they straggled on.

Charlie was heading south, then west around the hill. Kodiaks and Himalayas, the tourist booklet said. Man-made caves in a hillside semicircle.

Charlie had made his choice deliberately. The lions were across from the restaurant, where people came and went, ate and lingered. Birds and giraffes were too popular.

The Bear Pits, Charlie had decided, might entice that shiest of wild animals—a murderer.

Flattening wet hair back from his forehead, he slogged on. Two slickered teenagers, hand in hand, laughed their way past him and splashed toward the exits. Otherwise, he was quite alone now as he approached the Reptile House.

That would have been more like it, he thought. There was enough light filtering through the gloom to show carved serpent heads and tortured writhing columns. In drained half tones of gray, it was as charming as a nest of rattlesnakes.

The right setting for a twisted mind, Charlie thought. But, long before the rain began, he had decided that the Reptile House was too public for the man he was going to confront.

Ignoring deep puddles he walked on. When the breeze whipped overhanging branches, Charlie did not pause but tucked the manila folder under his arm.

The squishing of his own shoes and the steady patpat of rain were the only sounds he could hear now that the last visitors had left. In the distance, he saw dark spots on the pockmarked pond. Except for the waterfowl riding out the storm, Charlie could have been alone.

He knew he was not.

Nevertheless, he did not look behind to see if he was being stalked.

The Bear Pits were not far . . .

"Knapp!" It was a whisper, not a shout.

Charlie stood quite still.

"Is that you, Knapp?" The voice came from up ahead.

Narrowing his eyes against the weather, Charlie barely made out the figure. Raincoated, with hat-brim down, it did not tell him much. But both hands, he could see, were jammed deep in trenchcoat pockets.

"I'm Knapp," he said, watching the hands.

The murderer hesitated.

"Did you bring it?"

In slow motion, Charlie reached for the folder and held it up. A few raindrops weren't going to hurt it now.

The shadowy figure closed the gap between them. As he moved, he took his left hand out of his pocket.

"Before I do anything," said Charlie flatly, "I want to see the color of your money."

Three more steps and the right hand was still out of sight.

"Show me what's in that envelope!"

Charlie stayed where he was. The murderer mirrored his immobility. Then, at last, the right hand began moving.

"Hold it!"

From behind the Lion House, from the road to the pond, from the wooded hill, came pounding feet. The air bubble enclosing Charlie and a murderer collapsed. "You're covered! Do you hear—?"

Rushing policemen swarmed past Charlie. They were almost in time.

Charlie was still clutching an empty envelope when one shot rang out.

There had been a gun in Richard Macnamara's right pocket. But, this time, he had used it on himself.

CHAPTER 21

"So you were right, Ben. Macnamara was the murderer. But I'm the one who did something. I offered to sell a non-existent memo to all three of them, and that's what flushed him."

Charlie Knapp was sitting high in the catbird seat and didn't care who knew it. As for being the Ad Hoc Committee's guest, well why shouldn't they buy him lunch? He had saved their bacon, hadn't he?

"Hey!" Tony Martinelli grudged no man hospitality. But as a matter of principle, he denied indebtedness whenever possible. Floating IOUs have a way of being called at the worst moments. "Sure, you tied it up in ribbon, but Ben had already fingered Macnamara."

"And we could have all died of old age waiting for Heyer to make an arrest," Charlie said combatively.

Elsie's sense of propriety was offended. "I am sure that the authorities had no intention of letting the matter rest there."

"It was simply a matter of time," Ben agreed. "Once you knew where to look, a financial investigation would have finished Macnamara."

"And meanwhile Alison would have been knocked off," said Charlie. "Come on, Ben, admit that my way sewed the whole thing up before the day was out."

"Your way involved a shooting match at the Zoo," Ben retorted. He was still flinching at echoes of that gunshot.

Charlie was unperturbed. "I didn't shoot anybody. And it's

not my fault if you've got a gun-happy maniac in Congress. If you ask me, it's a good thing Macnamara killed himself."

He received a surprising amount of support.

"Quick and clean, that's the only way," said Tony, sawing the air energetically with his hands.

"If Dick Macnamara had been taken alive, we'd have had to continue the hearings." Lou Flecker shuddered.

"With our principal witness in handcuffs," Val chimed in.

"Tragic as the result has been," Mrs. Hollenbach intoned, "it will act as a deterrent to the next public servant who considers selling his vote."

Two drinks and Elsie saw potential backsliders everywhere.

Ben surveyed the table. "You're a bunch of bloodthirsty ghouls," he said without rancor.

"We're peaceable-minded legislators," countered Val Oakes. "Skip the lecture, Ben. You want to get elected this November every bit as much as we do. Tell us how you lit on Macnamara."

"It wasn't all that hard. After I spent the morning at police headquarters, I got complaints that people hadn't been able to reach me."

"Happens every time you leave your office," Val observed.

"Right," said Ben. "So how could Shirley Knapp call Macnamara from the airport? When he was out most of the afternoon? First he was at some convention, then he went on to a private party."

Four agile minds reviewed Macnamara's testimony. Charlie Knapp did not bother. "Maybe a secretary tracked him down," he objected. "Anyone can make a mistake about a telephone call."

"No." Ben amplified: "This was no ordinary phone call. If other people had been involved, Heyer would have heard about them. It was an outright lie. And once that started me looking at Macnamara, his guilt smacked me in the face."

Elsie Hollenbach was not prepared to tolerate any suggestion that she had overlooked the obvious. "How can you say that, Ben? We began with the disclosure of Shirley Knapp's memo and three men whose votes on Section C were critical. Then one of them shot Mrs. Knapp to protect himself. Surely, they were equally suspect."

"That's true except that you're starting in the wrong place. As

I told Heyer the real beginning was eighteen months ago when the bribe changed hands."

"But that didn't tell you whose hands, did it?" asked Flecker.

"Look, the murderer took the bribe for a reason—"

"Sure. Fifty thousand smackers worth of reason," Tony interrupted with gusto.

Ben saw that he would have to be more specific. "Val, remember watching Shirley Knapp operate at the NPA cocktail party? She was feminine one minute, then a backslapper and then an economist. She really studied her approach shots."

Val agreed. "That's why she was worth her weight in gold to the NPA."

Charlie looked into the past. "Shirley was winding people around her little finger when she was twenty years old," he said reminiscently.

"Exactly. And she put just as much skill into bribery, as the testimony at our hearings showed. Mrs. Knapp didn't simply wave fifty thousand dollars around. She dug out what people really wanted, then tempted them with their heart's desire. If anybody voting on Section C had wanted an oceangoing sloop so much he could taste it, she wouldn't have offered him cash. She would have told him the NPA happened to have a sloop to spare."

To a man reared in a parsonage, the text was irresistible. "Satan, get thee behind me," Val Oakes said majestically. When his companions merely stared, he said virtuously, "If you people read the Good Book more, you'd think of these things for yourselves."

Only Tony was without false pride. "How does it go on?" he asked with real curiosity.

"Tony, you can read it when you get back to your hotel," said Ben, anxious to sidestep theology. "Look how Shirley handled our three black sheep. You didn't need second sight to realize what Adelman wanted. So she offered him a high-powered staff that could make him a household name in New York. With Warren Praeger, it was easier still. The NPA would have enabled Praeger to be a big help to the right people back home. That would have put him in good with the regular organization and the Nebraska election would have stopped looking so black. But Dick Macnamara was a case apart. He wanted to maintain a real home in Massachusetts, while living in Washington. That meant keeping up two establishments, ferrying his family back and forth, supporting a lot of civic causes."

Frowning, Elsie Hollenbach reached a conclusion. "You mean, Macnamara was the only one who wanted ready cash?"

"That's one of the things I mean," Ben rejoined. "By his own admission, he was the only one offered a lump sum. And that fits in with Shirley Knapp's memo. She told Carrington she was taking fifty thousand out of the slush fund. If it had been Adelman, there would have been regular payments on leases and payrolls. With Praeger, the payoff would also have been on the installment plan. But Macnamara needed money he could spend to meet the monthly bills."

Elsie was fair. "Yes, we should have seen that."

Ben was sorry to have to add: "We overlooked something a lot bigger."

Val had cottoned on some time ago. "Eighteen months," he said self-accusingly. "And what did they have to show for it?"

"Christ!" Tony Martinelli struck his forehead dramatically. "It stands out like a sore thumb."

Ben grinned. "We were chumps. If Adelman had accepted Mrs. Knapp's offer a year and a half ago, why was he still obscure? If Warren Praeger was getting powerful backing, why did his opponent have such a good chance of unseating him? Macnamara was the boy who had what he wanted—and he'd gotten it some time ago."

Charlie Knapp was the only one who had nothing to blame himself for.

"You mean it's that simple?" he demanded. "Well, what have you been doing all this time? Why didn't you simply audit all three of them?"

Even Elsie Hollenbach, who could account for every penny she spent, blanched. "By and large, we hesitate to ask how a congressman spends his money," she murmured.

"We sure do!" Tony said.

Disregarding Charlie's expression, Ben continued: "Anyway, if Adelman or Praeger had been our meat, a standard audit wouldn't have uncovered the irregularities. That's what made Macnamara so vulnerable as soon as Alison proved the authenticity of the memo. Until then, the NPA was concentrating on keeping its own image clean. Both Shirley and Carrington were working on it, in their own ways. But once it was proved that a bribe had occurred, the game changed overnight. Carrington showed that by his call to Shirley in the hospital. Basically, he was telling her to come up with some foolproof plan to take the heat off, or the NPA would admit everything."

"Throwing her to the wolves," muttered Charlie, whose interview with John Carrington still rankled.

"Not quite as bad as that," Ben corrected. "Carrington was being realistic. The NPA would have liked to claim it was pure as the driven snow. But basically, everyone expects pressure groups to funnel money through channels. That isn't what makes people mad. Because it's not dangerous as long as legislators are honest. If everyone voting on Section C had been incorruptible, Shirley Knapp wouldn't have been a menace. When something like this bribe breaks, it's the crooked congressman the public wants to crucify."

There were four approving grunts. On this subject, honest congressmen feel even more strongly.

"Carrington knew that the smartest move for the NPA was to hand over the man they'd bought. Of course it would be rough on Shirley and finish her career in Washington. But that was a price he was willing to pay."

"I'll bet." Charlie hated to see the NPA president let off so lightly. "You make Carrington sound above it all. But Shirley could have tied him in to the bribe. And I can tell you, she was steaming when she checked out of the hospital. So he had plenty to lose, didn't he?"

"Look, Charlie, just because you dislike Carrington doesn't mean he's crazy," Ben answered. "Shirley may have been furious and she may have made last-ditch attempts to save herself, but her whole future depended on Carrington. In the long run, she would have calmed down and she would have done what they all do. She would have arranged her story to protect Carrington and to get immunity by naming Macnamara. Then there would have been an enormous outcry, Macnamara would have gone to jail and Shirley Knapp would have dropped out of sight. Only a few people would know that she was being taken care of nicely in Houston by a grateful Carrington."

Even Charlie knew too much about politics to argue. It was Tony who carried the discussion further.

"Once Carrington called her in Newburg, Shirley should have gotten on to the guy she bribed."

Val Oakes was pensive. "Those three jokers agreed that she was burning to work someone over by the time she reached National Airport."

"Earlier than that," Ben amended. "Charlie's told us she was going strong when she was still at the hospital. More important, he told us she called someone from the restaurant where they stopped. Logically three identical phone calls never made sense. Shirley would have made a very different call to the man she bribed. She had an emergency to talk to him about. So she called him from Ohio and demanded he meet her at the Washington airport."

"You can't be sure of that," Elsie pointed out.

"Well, we know Macnamara couldn't get a call from her after she was airborne. Yet he knew when she was landing and where she'd be. Furthermore he had a gun with him. Just think about the timetable for a minute, Elsie. The murderer really couldn't have gotten going on the basis of Shirley's Washington calls. Shirley wouldn't hang around for hours at the airport. The meeting must have been arranged beforehand. And Macnamara's program for the day tells you he was the man."

"Wait a minute, Ben," said Lou Flecker. "They all changed their schedules that day."

"At the last minute, with a lot of dislocation. If Adelman and Praeger had had hours' notice, they wouldn't have been caught short. They disrupted dinner parties and weekend plans on the spur of the moment—that is, after Shirley called from National. Macnamara was the one who had time to decide to attend a convention, get lost in a private party and go home to a house he knew was empty on Friday afternoons. And, I'll tell you something else about those phone calls. Macnamara wasn't saying anything until he was clued in by the others."

"Now, give the devil his due, Ben," Oakes cautioned. "Warren wasn't saying anything either until Adelman spilled the beans."

Ben was ahead of him. "It's true Praeger kept mum about that call until Adelman's press conference. But afterwards he was willing to describe it. Macnamara was in a bind. He didn't want to single himself out as being the only one not to receive a call. But he had no idea what Shirley said to the two who were innocent. So he had to let Praeger do all the work, then agreed that his call had been exactly the same. He was so determined to hide behind the other two that he overlooked a glaring discrepancy—at five o'clock he wasn't anywhere Shirley could have reached him."

Tony Martinelli always took bright interest in his fellow human beings, no matter what they were up to. "What do you suppose Shirley and Macnamara talked about at the airport? Or did he just take out his shooter and let her have it?"

"Who knows? At least they talked their way to her car. It can't have been easy for either of them. Macnamara said they hadn't seen each other since the day she offered him the bribe. And he was probably telling the truth—except that it was the day he *took* the bribe." Ben fell silent, finding it impossible to visualize that encounter.

"Yes," Elsie said slowly. "Dick Macnamara would have avoided her. No doubt, by the time the *Post* published her memo, he had suppressed the whole incident."

"He bent over backward," Ben reflected. "Herb Adelman said he had a hard time cutting Shirley off. But he never claimed that he didn't bump into her at parties. But Macnamara was adamant that he never saw her again. He took great care not to."

"That Adelman!" said Lou. "He's a smart cookie, all right. He's organizing a drive for stricter regulation of lobbyists. You mark my words, we're going to see an Adelman Bill before he's done."

Tony reached into personal history. "Got a lot of energy, that kid," he said tolerantly. "He's not going to have any trouble getting re-elected. Hell, he latches onto anything passing by . . ."

Hyattsville had left no scars on Congressman Martinelli.

"Then he's the one person to emerge unscathed," Elsie Hollenbach sniffed. "Because Warren Praeger is certainly going to be swept out of office."

"Yes, yes," everyone murmured sycophantically.

It had been a black day for Elsie when she discovered that

Warren Praeger and his doctor lived in the same building. Her colleagues were still treading cautiously.

Even Charlie Knapp scented danger.

"And what about that Underwood dame?" he asked quickly. "The one who came out to the house when Billy was there. What was she after?"

Ben suddenly burst out laughing. "You'll never guess. She finally was well enough to tell Heyer, and he's still gnashing his teeth about it."

"Yes?" prompted Val.

"She was after Shirley's job."

"But she wasn't interested in her work," Martinelli protested. "She was the home-and-hearth girl."

"Up to a point. Then a lot of things happened all at once."

"Yeah," said Charlie sourly. "Like a murder."

"That's not what got her going. Suddenly she found herself doing things she'd never done before and she liked feeling important. And Carrington didn't help. From what Heyer says, he pulls the Texas charm in the office. Mrs. Underwood got the wrong idea. She thought he was impressed with her competence. And she was clever enough to see that locating the murderer would get the NPA off the hook. She convinced herself that if she could just produce the right scrap of paper, she'd become a big time NPA lobbyist."

Val Oakes was not often startled after a lifetime in Washington. "And that's all she had to go on?"

"Absolutely. Barbara Underwood hoped Shirley had written down details of the bribe because it was the only way her dream could come true. But the very silliness of her behavior made it dangerous. Macnamara had as much trouble as you do, Val, believing it was pie in the sky. She had already circled around Praeger and Adelman. The last thing she remembers is starting for Macnamara's office. That must have been the final straw. I expect he followed her and grabbed at the chance to leave a body on the NPA doorstep."

Tony Martinelli had a good memory. "Macnamara always tried making himself look good at someone else's expense. Like the way he teamed up with Praeger at first so that Adelman was the loner."

"And then he pulled a switch immediately after Praeger's bad showing," Ben expanded. "I found him buddying up to Adelman in the Carlton."

Val Oakes was still bemused by Barbara Underwood. "Does Carrington know that little lady threw half of Washington into a tizzy because she was after Shirley Knapp's salary? Or hasn't Heyer told him?"

"Carrington knows. And he's reacting just the way you'd expect. He's sent half a florist's shop to the hospital and he's airfreighted someone up from Houston to be the NPA's new man."

"It would be more to the point," said Elsie Hollenbach, "if John Carrington air-freighted himself back to Houston."

Ben was suitably grave. "I understand that he's planning to retire from the NPA. On grounds of health."

Lou Flecker snorted while Tony said: "God help Texas."

Charlie Knapp had decided this whole recital proved that he was right. "Macnamara sounds as if he was around the bend by the time I got to him. It's a damn good thing he didn't get to run wild any more."

In a way, Ben had to agree. "The beginning spoiled him. He got his money, no questions were raised, and he was able to forget the whole episode. Then the roof fell in. Alison leaked the memo and, before Macnamara knew where he was at, he was standing over Shirley with a smoking revolver. From then on, he acted half crazy. Let's put it this way, Charlie. I'm glad Alison didn't cross his path during the last few days."

Modesty was not Charlie's line. "That's what I kept saying," he reiterated. "I'll be glad to see the last of this town."

Elsie recalled that this was a farewell lunch. "You're leaving today, aren't you?"

"Billy and I are catching the four-thirty plane. Everything's worked out okay. Alison's moving in with two other girls. And I got a pretty good deal on the house. Managed to sell the contents to the same people." Charlie's lips quirked into a grin. "Even that lawyer is satisfied."

"Perhaps it's just as well," Elsie said wisely, "if Alison doesn't come to Newburg with you."

Charlie recognized an oblique question. "No sweat. Alison's going to spend a couple weeks with us next September. I finally got it out of her. She was hit hard by Shirley's murder, you know. She was scared it was her fault and worked herself into a state. But I got her to see that she wasn't responsible. Shirley started it all and Macnamara finished it."

Elsie voiced crisp approval. A load of guilt, she said, was too heavy a burden for a nineteen-year-old girl.

"Maybe I went too far," Charlie confessed. "I tried getting her to take something of Shirl's to this new apartment of hers. But she said she didn't want anything to remind her. She'll be sorry some day."

"As long as she's okay now, that's the important thing," Ben said bracingly.

"Well, you can see for yourself. As soon as she's finished moving her junk, she'll be picking me up."

And twenty minutes later Alison Knapp did rush into the restaurant, flushed from her exertions, but otherwise in radiant spirits.

"I'm only two blocks from campus," she said, accepting a cup of coffee. "Oh, and Charlie, I thought it over while the boys were packing the books. And I decided to take that little walnut sewing table of Mother's, the one where she kept her needlepoint."

It was an unexpected insight into Shirley Knapp's leisure hours. Charlie looked pleased but prudently said nothing.

"After all," said Alison, faintly embarrassed, "Mother wasn't so bad."

And that, Val Oakes told Ben Safford after their guests departed, was one hell of an epitaph for a lobbyist.